Anil Chopra was born in New Delhi and grew up in Mussoorie with his guardian, the author, Ruskin Bond. After finishing medical school, he went to Great Britain to practice medicine and later emigrated to the United States where he lives with his wife and two children.

Unforeseen Desires

ANIL CHOPRA

Foreword by RUSKIN BOND

SPEAKING TIGER

SPEAKING TIGER PUBLISHING PVT. LTD
4381/4, Ansari Road, Daryaganj
New Delhi 110002

First published in India by Speaking Tiger in paperback 2017

ISBN: 978-93-86338-71-6
eISBN: 978-93-86338-72-3

10 9 8 7 6 5 4 3 2 1

Typeset in Sabon Roman by SÜRYA, New Delhi
Printed at Thomson Press India Ltd.

This is a work of fiction. Names, characters, places and incidents either are the product of the author's imagination or are used fictitiously, and any resemblance to actual persons, living or dead, events or locales is entirely coincidental.

For Ruskin Bond
who taught me to think in English

For
Bably, Yash, Sheetal and my mother

'An open sin is only half a sin, and a secret innocence is only half innocent.'

—Graham Greene

Foreword

Although Anil took up medicine as a profession, his heart was always in literature. During the four years he lived with me in Mussorie (1965–69), he attended Wynberg-Allen School as a day-scholar. I was then living in Maplewood Lodge, a small cottage below the school's playing field.

Wynberg-Allen had several good English teachers—Colin Carr, Jeremy Firth (both of whom had come out from England) and our own Doreas Edwardes from Lucknow—and Anil certainly benefitted from their teaching. It wasn't long before he had gone through most of my own modest library. Biographies of great men of medicine such as Pasteur, Lister and others might well have influenced his choice of career. And his favourite novels have clearly inspired him to write one of his own, which paints a nostalgic picture of Dehradun and Mussoorie of the 1970s, and gives a sensitive account of a young man's coming of age.

I was not closely involved in Anil's life during the period he describes in this novel, and for many years he has lived abroad with his family. But he has always stayed in touch, and it is good to know that he has finally found time to give expression to his literary talents. All glory comes from daring to begin!

Ruskin Bond

24 February 2017

I

He stood in a corner with his arms behind his back. The hospital Superintendent had her back towards him as she gazed out of the window to the premature monsoon clouds and orange sunlight that cast misshapen shadows across the valley. Across her desk lay ill-stacked files which smelled of forgotten dust storms, tied together with coloured strings. On top of the pile stood the brass statue of goddess Durga, which she used as a paperweight.

Above her head hung the smiling portrait of Mrs Indira Gandhi, who had declared a state of Emergency in the country. Billboards advertising her recent population-control drive—a man and a woman with two smiling children under the slogan: Hum Do, Humare Do—were everywhere. There was an air of urgency to put the country right, and the wheels of governmental bureaucracy were in a frenzy of efficiency and moral righteousness. Trains ran on time. People came to work on time. There was less litter on the streets. The atmosphere was full of fear and apprehension, and people stayed away from the streets.

When she turned around, her face had a sour expression, he thought, the puffiness of freshly baked sourdough bread that comes with middle age. Silently, she walked towards the fresh intern, Arun. She seemed to weigh him with her still eyes. The tousle of his black hair lay lazily over his forehead, and the youthful dazzle of his eyes and a dimple on his cheek gave him a schoolboyish innocence.

Looks can be deceptive, she thought. Judging from what he had claimed to the Matron earlier, he had no idea where the diamond rings had disappeared. Pointing her finger below his nose she said, 'I want Dr Gupta's wedding rings back, otherwise you will never see your completion certificate. How could you do such a thing?' She paused, chewing on her glasses. 'Mind you, I have had surprises from interns of so-called good families.' Then she dangled her glasses like a pendulum in front of his eyes and in an urgent voice said, 'Is that clear, Doctor?'

He was in a daze. A rush of blood came to his cheeks; he buttoned his white coat and turned around to leave her office. Once more he heard behind him, 'Is that absolutely clear?'

He retraced his steps from the previous afternoon—after the rings went missing. He had ridden his bicycle on the gravel path to the tea shop, which stood under the ancient banyan tree outside the hospital boundary wall. Under the brilliant sun, he hoped to see the glint of gold somewhere on the gravel. It seemed as futile as his childhood quest when he would gaze up into the night sky, hoping to see a shooting star, to make a wish.

There was nothing under the bench in the tea shop where had taken off his blood-stained white coat and secured it to the carrier of his bike. Walking back to the hospital, he scoured the earth beneath his feet for those diamond wedding rings. Nothing.

He had met Dr Nasreen Gupta as her intern for the first time the previous morning, when she had conducted an unexpected delivery. Her name seemed incongruous. Nasreen evoked Persian lineage. Her married name, Gupta, was a run-of-the-mill name. If distilled beauty were the sum of proportional features and mental agility, then Nasreen, even with the scar on her upper lip, seemed the essence, a Wild Rose as her name suggested. She had a feminine poise. Her gleaming eyes, even in the face of terror, seemed engaging. She had driven in the early hours of the morning to meet with the Superintendent, and had been crying in her office.

'Do you know what that means for me? Do you know that my mother-in-law will kill me if she finds out I have lost my wedding rings in the first year of my marriage?' her voice trailed almost to a whisper, like a calm before the storm. She leaned against the pillar for support. 'It is a bad omen,' she sobbed, 'a bad, bad omen. Don't you remember? I gave them to you in the operating room.'

He distinctly remembered the moment she had given him those rings the previous morning. Thereafter there were only waves of swirling memory that rose and fell: the flashes of anxious faces, the smell of the disinfectant in the delivery room, the clamour of surgical instruments on shuddering carts. The face of the pregnant sixteen-year-old girl had haunted him all night. She was in the late stages of labour. Rivulets of sweat formed in the strands of her hair, her face pale and exhausted in anticipation of the next cramp. She lay there with her legs apart, until there was an eruption of blood from inside her.

'Open the IV to full, Dr Arun,' Dr Gupta commanded as she swung around and grabbed a pair of gloves, took off her wedding rings and handed them to him. After putting on her gloves, she made a fist, thrusting her knuckles in between the girl's legs to stop the bleeding.

A pool of blood had formed on the floor. The nurse could not feel the pulse or record the blood pressure. In those tense moments, the nurses acted before Dr Gupta could give instructions. Someone hung up the blood transfusion bag, others wheeled in the emergency cart. Arun put the oxygen mask on the girl's face. He could not bear to see more blood pouring out at the end of the table—the head-end seemed to be the safest place. He could see the desperation on Dr Gupta's face as she tried to stop the deluge of fresh, warm blood with its metallic odour. There were voices, not directed to anyone in particular, just floating phrases—'Oh, she is getting cold and blue', 'She has stopped breathing'. The voices became stronger and urgent, instructions were relayed as if from a well-rehearsed protocol.

The girl was no longer in agony as she turned paler, and blue at the lips. Her legs splayed open as she became limp and cold, her chest still. There was an unforgiving silence, which seemed interminably long until it was broken by the cry of the newborn baby. Dr Gupta quickly clamped the cord. The young nurse carefully wrapped the slippery baby in dry towels.

Arun stood motionless, staring at the spent syringes. He felt Dr Gupta's rings in his pocket. He took them out to put them on the surgical tray in front of Dr Gupta and thought of quietly slipping away. There was someone knocking at the door. No one moved towards it. The knocking became louder. Dr Gupta took off her bloodied coat and surgical gloves. 'Arun, don't let anyone in. I will speak with the relatives in a few minutes,' said Dr Gupta as she sat on the stool cupping her face with her hands.

❖

Nasreen looked at her long, slender fingers and felt almost naked without the wedding rings. Surely, Dr Arun could not have lost them just like that. She could not believe he had the audacity to smile and simply say, 'I do not have them. I really don't.' She wept all the way as she drove home in her Fiat. She hoped her mother-in-law would not notice her bare hands; she always took the rings off before kneading the dough. Ramu, the teenage servant, usually prepared everything else and her mother-in-law was very particular about cleanliness. Although she made him wash his hands before cooking, sometimes repeatedly, she never let him knead the dough. If Nasreen was at work, her mother-in-law would take it upon herself to knead the flour even though it made her breathless.

The culture here was so different from Bombay where she grew up, thought Nasreen.

Her mother was a Parsi convent schoolteacher who was widowed at a young age. She never employed a servant, unlike everyone else around her, as a matter of principle. How could one human being have authority over another? She was a believer in Gandhian principles. Nasreen had faint memories of her father, who always drove around wearing a hat. She was five years old when he died. One afternoon, she returned from school to her home, a rambling ancestral bungalow at Four Bungalows by the sea, and heard all the tenants wailing.

It was a chance meeting with Rakesh on Marine Drive in Bombay that had led to her betrothal. He had fallen off a scooter when her car neared the scene of the accident. He was in a daze and seemed to be walking towards the oncoming traffic. She stopped her car, causing a traffic jam behind her, and gave him a ride to his hotel nearby in Colaba. According to the three tenets of Zoroastrianism that she had grown up with—good thoughts, good words and good deeds—she felt bound to help him.

'Are you sure you don't want to go to the hospital?' she had asked him.

'I am fine. I was just not myself for a few seconds after the initial shock. I thought someone might run over me... no one bothered to stop except for you.'

'I think it is a concussion, but really you should be observed for head injury. I am a doctor. My hospital is nearby.'

'I am so pleased to meet you, er, Dr...'

'Nasreen Munshee.'

'I am Rakesh Gupta from, a small town, Dehradun.' She smiled. He noticed her perfectly aligned teeth underneath the scar of harelip surgery, which showed the edges of her beautiful upper teeth every time she smiled. Her serene eyes, with long eyelashes, did not let one to linger on her upper lip.

'I like small towns,' she said, flicking her hair away from her cheek.

'Strangely, I love big cities.'

They met again. In the next few months, Rakesh sought every opportunity to visit Bombay. Their friendship blossomed because of their love of books and performing arts. One evening, when the sun was setting, after seeing a dance performance at the Radio Club, Rakesh proposed to her.

'I am Parsi. I hope your mother knows that.'

'I hope your mother knows I am a non-practicing Hindu. But we have something in common,' he said as he took her hand.

'Like what, may I ask?' she smiled.

'We both do not have siblings and we both live with widowed mothers.'

The wedding rings he had ordered for her were, in fact, two rings. Each had half a heart set in diamond. When worn, the two rings clicked together to form a full heart with gleaming diamonds in the middle. The diamonds were given to him by his mother.

As she drove back to the house, she could not remember

why she had chosen to wear her rings to work today of all days. She knew her mother-in-law didn't approve of the marriage, but Nasreen loved Rakesh. Even after almost a year of marriage, he had never alluded to her harelip surgery. Her mother-in-law had asked if her children would be affected, if and when she got pregnant. The day the young girl died in childbirth, her memory was in a haze. Perhaps Arun had given back the rings, and she had misplaced them somewhere. All she had wanted to do after that horrific afternoon was to sleep, a sleep so deep as to forget the stare of the girl and the puffs of warm air rising from the bloodied towels.

❖

The tea shop by the roadside had been Arun's refuge. It began to rain, and soon there was a ferocious downpour, as it was the monsoon season. The hospital building, which had seen better days during the British Raj, had a greenish hue from the moss-covered walls. Plants sprouted from the most unlikely places—drainpipes, gutters, windowsills and ledges. At the tea shop, he saw the two nurses who had been in the operating room that day. They quickly turned their faces as if to hide a secret. One of them had held him in her gaze through the surgical mask when the girl had died.

'May I join you?' he asked.

They looked at each other, but did not reply. He sat down anyway. They looked pretty in their starched white uniforms and blue-and-white bonnets. He ordered his usual glass of tea. 'So what did you do with those rings?' one of them asked.

'I lost them.'

'That's not what the Superintendent thinks.'

'I have got to go, Trishna,' said her friend, and hurriedly got up to leave.

'So you are Trishna from the OR?'

'Trishnapalli,' she corrected him.

'Do you think I sold them or something?'

'No, I don't,' she said. 'The Superintendent says Delhi boys from rich families can do anything...even drugs.' She tilted her head as if to straighten her bonnet, and pursed her lips. Somehow, she was not sure about his character.

She had moved to this small government hospital in the foothills of the Himalayas from a large city hospital in Agra. After a year-long relationship with a doctor, she had discovered he was married. She found the culture here, in north India, quite different from her home in the southern state of Kerala. She missed home but was happy to have a job and a place of her own in the nurses' hostel.

'Do be careful with the Superintendent,' she cautioned Arun. 'She is very fond of Dr Gupta. You'd better find those wedding rings.'

He noticed she wore a pendant of Lord Shiva, which rested just above her cleavage. Her black eyes were set symmetrically in a perfectly oval face. She smelled of sandalwood and incense, mixed with the odour of the delivery room. They ordered some more tea and watched the traffic go by. Arun had youthful acceptance that made even ennui seem comforting—drinking tea lazily by the roadside, waiting for buses that never seemed to arrive—because life's highway seemed to stretch far into the horizon. Trishna reminded him to ask the tea vendor if he had found any gold rings. Of course he had not seen any gold rings, not in his busy tea shop frequented by all sorts of people, including the girls from the degree college not far from the hospital.

2

Arun cycled towards Rajpur Road. On this road were the estates of the elite. Hidden behind big gates adorned with bougainvillea creepers were lush green lawns with groves of litchi trees. He loved to ride his bike on this deserted road. There was never much traffic except for the tourist taxis to Mussoorie. Beyond, he could see the distinctive Camel's Back outline of the peaks of Mussoorie shrouded in mist. It was a respite to get away from the hospital. Lately he had worried so much about the lost rings that when he walked or rode his bike, he always had his eyes on the ground. He turned his bike to the path leading to the old Methodist Church. Further, the path disappeared into an orchard of litchi trees. Beyond the trees stood an old colonial bungalow with a verandah. There was a small sign at the entrance that read: The Language School.

Perhaps he could learn French or German, he thought. A flock of parrots, like a green sheet, shot up from the trees against the blue sky, and then a swarm of bees surrounded him. He ran for his life until he reached the front door. A squadron of bees had stung him on his face. Breathless, he knocked at the door. A petite Englishwoman in a summer dress opened the door. Her intense blue eyes, set in a pale face with freckles, exaggerated her startled look.

'Hello, how may I help you?' Her hello sounded like hell-low, stiff with formal cordiality as she half-closed the door.

'I have been stung by the bees in your garden.'

'So you need to see a doctor?' She closed the door further.

'I am a doctor...Madam.'

'Oh, you look too young to be a doctor. For heaven's sake, come in. Your face is swelling up.'

On the walls of the colonial bungalow were portraits of Jesus on the cross, and some with his chest open, showing his heart with a halo around it. In the corner, stood a grand mahogany piano with a Tiffany lamp on top. He wondered why the language school had so many portraits of Jesus everywhere. The lady had been listening to the world service of the BBC. A Grundig radio stood on the table broadcasting the latest news: 'This is the Far Eastern relay station of the BBC... Now the news read by Ted Baker. There has been widespread opposition to Mrs Indira Gandhi's emergency rule. This morning, she arrested...'

The lady switched off the radio, straightened her short blonde hair, and tried to decide where to seat him. She momentarily lifted her arm towards the little stool near the piano.

'So, how can I help you, Doctor?'

'I would like to learn a foreign language such as German or French at your language school.'

'Well. Well. I have never had this request before,' she said, half smiling. 'We teach Hindi to the folks who come from overseas to spread the Gospel.'

He was suddenly at a loss for words. He looked out of the window and saw a banyan tree across the lawn. Behind the banyan tree stood a small apartment building under the shade of eucalyptus trees.

'You have a beautiful place here, so peaceful. Except for the bees,' he laughed.

The thought of cycling back to the hospital irked him.

He wished he could live in this oasis, this Garden of Eden, with the towering mountains in the backdrop. It was a stark contrast to his small room next to the medical ward from where he could hear the coughs of the patients suffering from tuberculosis. He mustered enough courage to ask her if she had any accommodation to spare for a stranger who was going to be in town only for a year, until he completed his internship.

'Not really,' she said. 'I am only a caretaker of the church property until I leave for England.'

Quite inconspicuously, a gaunt-looking man appeared, carrying a wooden tray with a glass of water on it, covered by a lace doily with hanging beads. Presumably, he was her khansamah, or her Man Friday. 'Water for the sahib?' he asked.

'Doctor Sahib,' she corrected him. From his nicotine-stained fingers and barrel-shaped chest, Arun could tell he was a smoker. The man disappeared into the corridor as unobtrusively as he had entered. He was there, but not quite there; unseen in the afternoon sunlight that filtered through the skylights in greyish-blue shafts.

'Well, I must take your leave. Although I do not fancy going back to the hospital,' he said with a smile.

'Do you really dislike the hospital accommodation so much?'

'Not so much the hospital accommodation. It is the added loneliness, I suppose. In the early hours of morning, I hear the cries of relatives who come to claim the bodies.'

'Oh, how awful!'

Was it her own loneliness because of which she could empathize, or her Christian belief, or her English politeness that prompted her to say this? He was not sure, but he felt happy he could talk to someone.

❖

As he cycled back, he had almost forgotten about Dr Gupta's wedding rings. He went past Astley Hall, the last shopping enclave created by the British before they left India. Here one could get Kwality's ice cream, ham, bacon and freshly baked bread. It had an aroma of sophistication, cleanliness and exclusivity. Beyond Astley Hall was the Clock Tower, which was really a roundabout that marked the beginning of Paltan Bazaar, an Indianization of Platoon Bazaar. Here the soldiers and cadets of the Defence Academy mingled with the general public. The bazaar always seemed full, even at midday; people walked up and down, or just stood in corners looking at nothing in particular. At the end of Paltan Bazaar, the road turned to the hospital.

Later that evening the hospital building looked tranquil surrounded by fading mountain peaks in the subdued purple twilight of the valley. The cottony air hung above the valley without any movement.

❖

Inside the emergency room a man lay gasping, shooting up his arms as if trying to pick cotton in the air. From the sweat on the man's brow and his bluish lips, Arun could tell the man was in *status asthamaticus*, a term that had stuck in his memory since the day he had first heard and read about it. The man was so short of breath that he was unable to give his name. The Matron was already rolling the oxygen cylinder towards him. Arun quickly secured a venous line and injected hydrocortisone, as he had been trained to do. This was the first time he was in charge, and this man's life depended on him. He held the man's hand, not just to comfort him but to feel his pulse: it was feeble and racing, definitely not a good sign. The oxygen mask was on his face, but his nails and lips were getting bluer, his forehead wrinkling into a stare of impending doom. Arun glanced at the gauge on top of the oxygen cylinder. To his horror, it read zero.

'Matron, please come here,' he shouted. 'Why is there no oxygen flowing? Why is this not connected properly?'

'May I have a word with you in private, Doctor?' said the plump middle-aged Matron with an air of authority. She had seen many enthusiastic interns pass through the hospital corridors over the years. She grabbed him by the arm and took him aside. 'There is no oxygen in the cylinder,' she whispered in his ear. 'The cylinder with oxygen in this hospital is being used in the operating room by Dr Mishra. Do you understand now?'

'No, I don't! You are trying to kill him by suffocating him with an empty oxygen mask!' A remark he regretted making as soon as he uttered it.

A male nurse might have punched him, but the Matron retreated and burst into tears. A bevy of younger nurses surrounded her, directing furtive glances at Arun as he went about taking off the mask and injecting some more hydrocortisone. Slowly, the man's lips turned pink, his chest was moving again and he was able to say, 'thank you'.

The emergency room was really a verandah that had been converted into a long room with little cubicles. It was called 'Casualty'. Indeed, one could easily become a casualty, not from lack of expertise but from lack of equipment. There were some exceptional physicians and non-physicians, that rare breed of paramedical staff who could just take a perfunctory look at a patient and make a diagnosis: 'Doctor Sahib, another dislocated shoulder.' The smell of chloroform, tincture of benzene, surgical spirits and boiling glass syringes exuded from the walls; the only things that glinted in the dimly lit rooms were the chrome auroscopes and vaginal colposcopes.

The night seemed long. The Matron busied herself in her corner without looking at Arun, still feeling unnerved by the impertinence of a raw intern questioning her authority. Occasionally, she checked the expiry dates of the intravenous fluid bags and rearranged the shelves full of vials, but most of the time she sat with the emergency room physician, Dr Thomas, who seemed unusually cheerful at this time of the night. He was a portly man wearing a belt with a shiny brass clip that constantly slipped from its equatorial girth. He sat at his desk reading the local paper and occasionally whistled to himself out of sheer boredom. Arun pretended to read the *Principles of Medicine* by Davidson, aware of the Matron's movements. A little later she carried in a tray of hot tea with only two cups.

'So, you are the new kid on the block,' said Dr Thomas, in his south-Indian accent. 'We have heard so much about you already, haven't we?'

'About me, Dr Thomas?'

'Yes, you know, everyone is talking about those wedding rings.'

The Matron gave him a sly look and walked towards the entrance to let in a couple with a baby in the young mother's arms.

'Please help us, Doctor Sahib. It is my first child. He hasn't eaten for two days and he is running a high fever.'

Arun noticed some pus coming out of the child's right ear. The child was listless with a vacant look and had a black mark on his forehead, to ward off evil spirits and the jealous gazes of barren women.

Dr Thomas hitched his trousers and turned to Arun. 'Come, come hold the baby in your arms. Don't be afraid. Tell me what is wrong with the baby?'

The mother looked terrified as Arun carefully took the baby from her arms. 'Dr Thomas, the diagnosis is obvious.

The child has a bad ear infection, *otitis media* to be precise,' he said confidently. The nurse smiled at Dr Thomas.

'Obvious! Obvious, yes, indeed. I liked the way he said "to be precise"; isn't that so, Sistar? There was a reason why I asked you to hold the baby. Isn't that so, Sistar?' He laughed. The nurse was already setting up a surgical tray. The mother looked on in anguish, not knowing what the doctor was about to do with the baby.

'When you picked up the baby, did you notice the way the baby was holding its head?' Dr Thomas laid the baby on his side. His large hand gently stroked the baby's head as if in awe of the smoothness of the head. 'Feel it, my friend,' he said, guiding Arun's hand to the baby's head, 'Bulging anterior fontanelle! Have you already forgotten your medicine?' He pushed a needle into the baby's spine and milky white fluid bubbled out. 'Meningitis, my friend. Nothing is obvious in medicine.'

After an hour or two of administering intravenous antibiotics, the baby was alert and kicking in its mother's arms. After two humbling experiences, Arun longed to be in his bed. He would not have to start working till midday. It was almost morning. Dr Thomas picked up his backpack to leave.

The Matron gave a triumphant smile to Dr Thomas, and Arun tried to catch her attention to say some soothing words to assuage the situation. But she had seen it all before, hardened with the sights of suffering and disease—the last stares of human beings at peril, young and old, their last gasps and their indignities. Her own face, accustomed to equanimity in every adversity, was now singularly austere of any softening creases she might have once possessed. She stared at him and said: 'I am sure the Superintendent would like to see you in her office sometime today.'

❖

When he woke up around noon, there was a knock on the door. It was a ward boy who informed him the Superintendent was waiting to see him in her office. Arun walked down the long corridor to her office. The rays of the sun felt almost damp as they filtered through the ground fog of the morning.

The Superintendent's meeting with the Matron and the surgeon, Dr Mishra, was about to conclude. 'What could I do, Dr Mishra? You were using the oxygen in the OR. At least I had the sense to calm the relatives by putting on the oxygen mask.'

'I understand, Matron. He will learn soon,' said the Superintendent. Dr Mishra, a tall middle-aged surgeon with a toothbrush moustache, who always seemed to be chewing scented betel nut, nodded in agreement. He nodded to everything the Superintendent said, afraid of being transferred to some outpost of the state.

When Arun entered the office, the Matron quickly took out a handkerchief and dabbed her eyes.

'So, you have been causing a lot of commotion in the Casualty, haven't you? Insulting the Matron, and that too in front of the relatives. Do you have any sense?' the Superintendent demanded.

'But, Madam, I was just practicing what I have been taught,' replied Arun.

'I am having none of that, you understand. What is taught in medical schools is not what we always practice but, more importantly, what we practice is not always what is taught to us. Medicine is not just knowledge; it is how you apply it in the real world. I want you to apologize to the Matron. Oxygen is in short supply in our hospital, in our country for that matter.'

'I am sorry, Madam,' said Arun.

'When do you rotate with me in surgery, my boy?' asked Dr Mishra.

'Next month, Sir.'

'You have a lot to learn, my boy,' he mumbled, chewing the betel nut, his cheeks now bulging with the saliva. He nodded to the Superintendent.

As soon as Dr Mishra left with the Matron, the Superintendent asked Arun if he had recovered the rings. When he said 'no', she shut the door. 'Well, I have a surprise for you. Dr Gupta's husband is a lawyer, a very prominent lawyer, if I may say so. He is curious to know what you did with his wife's wedding rings. He wants to meet you.'

Arun was too tired to understand anything. Dr Gupta hadn't been seen in the hospital after losing her rings. If only he could talk to her again.

'So, when did you last see the rings?'

Arun did not answer immediately, trying to remember. Then in a tired voice he said, 'In the delivery room when she handed them to me.'

'Where did you go after you left the delivery room?' Arun looked out of the window. He could see the tea shop across the road. 'I walked to the tea shop, just to be by myself after the young girl died.'

'When you paid for the tea, didn't you feel the rings in your pockets?'

'No.'

'So, you supposedly lost them between the delivery room and the tea shop.'

'I must have. I don't remember anything from the time she gave them to me.'

The Superintendent looked at him sceptically. 'Let me tell you something, Mister. This might jog your weak memory. Dr Gupta is very depressed because of you, do you understand? Try and remember what happened.'

After the Superintendent dismissed Arun from her office, she tried to call Dr Gupta at home, but there was no answer. She wondered why Nasreen, a Parsi, had married Mr Gupta in the first place. It was all in the stars, she supposed. Yes, all in the stars, as she herself had missed three chances of getting married, due to no fault of her own, but it happened every time, and she could not blame anyone or anything, except her horoscope. Perhaps Nasreen was never meant to wear those rings. Was it not in the stars that the young girl had to die on the table in childbirth? Dr Arun probably lost the rings on the hospital grounds, and the chances of someone returning them, with so many Class IV employees, were very slim.

She opened her cupboard to look into the mirror behind the door. Her eyebrows had overgrown like an unkempt hedge, and some hair had sprouted on her forehead. There was a band of white in her head of hair, just like Mrs Indira Gandhi, whom she admired. She wondered if it might be appropriate to send Dr Arun to the sterilization camps around town, where there was a shortage of medical personnel, and keep him away from Dr Gupta for a while.

3

Sujata was the only female intern in their group of four. She was tall and lithe, with short hair. Her upturned nose and green eyes could easily belie her Indianness. She was always cheerful and full of humour, but beneath her perpetual pleasant personality, as it often happens, floated the unexpected dregs that life often tosses. Her fifteen-year-old brother was almost blind from optic atrophy. She had that maturity which comes with unwarranted responsibility.

Ever since her brother began to lose his vision, she had a way with eyes. They were the mirrors of one's character, and she could read them with a glance. Sodi, the tall Sikh intern from a military family, like her, gave her lascivious looks, and when she stared back at him, he would pretend he was adjusting his turban. She noted his looks were not exclusively for her but also for the well-rounded cleaning women in the hospital corridors.

Rana, the intern from Sainj Khat village, was short and bespectacled, with a sulky face and an air of arrogance, which did not serve him well. He probably got into medical school because of some political background. He claimed his grandfather was a freedom fighter.

Arun was from Delhi, and from his eyes she could tell he was not hiding any secrets. She did not believe the rumours circulating in the hospital that he had got rid of Dr Gupta's wedding rings even for a moment. She liked his voice and the way he talked.

When she saw him coming out of the Superintendent's office, looking a little lost, she called after him. 'Don't look so glum. It is not the end of the world, you know.'

'I am so tired, that's all, and before you ask me anything else...like about the wedding rings...' he snapped.

'Silly you! That is not what I had on my mind. Do you want to go to the movies at Picture Palace?'

'What is showing?'

'*Dr Zhivago*! A really romantic movie,' she said with glee.

'I heard it is very long. I will probably fall asleep after my horrendous night on call.'

'Doesn't matter. I can always tell you the story later, like I do for my brother. He loves to have someone read to him. He was an avid reader before he lost his vision,' she said wistfully.

'I would love to read to him,' said Arun, feeling sympathetic. 'What kind of books does he like?'

'Oh, adventure stories mostly. He loved *Mutiny on the Bounty*. I like romantic stories. I have a collection of Ruskin Bond's short stories, and I really liked this story about a blind girl. It's called "The Eyes Have It". Maybe you can read it to him.'

'Why would your brother like to listen to a story about a blind girl?'

'Why not? My brother has a very positive attitude. You will see when you meet him.'

The movie was indeed long enough to put Arun to sleep. He enjoyed the music more than the movie. In the scene where Dr Zhivago gets off the tram, the last time he sees Lara walking away and clutches his chest, Sujata grasped Arun's arm and dug her fingernails into his flesh. Arun turned towards her and saw her liquescent eyes glistening in the glare of the screen. The sound suddenly became muffled as heavy rain pounded on the roof. The dialogue became inaudible and the roof began to leak. Some resourceful patrons simply opened their umbrellas and did not budge.

'Let us go to Kwality's and have some coffee before we go home,' said Sujata.

Arun was a little nervous about going to her house for the first time and meeting her mother and brother. He was very hungry, and it had been a long time since he had eaten home-cooked food. 'Is your mother a good cook?'

'Oh my god. She is the best. She makes the best rajma-chawal in the world. Do you know, she only buys the best basmati rice that grows in the village called Tapovan, where Dronacharya apparently came for penance after the great war of Mahabharta,' she said stirring her coffee and playing with the spoon as if another thought was stirring in her mind.

'Is your family in Delhi?'

'No. My family is in England. My brothers and sisters, along with my mother, left four years ago to join my father. It is a long story. I stayed behind to complete my medical school.'

'Oh. Will you go to England to join them?'

'Possibly.'

'Hop on the pillion, time for a nice drive on my Lambretta.'

They rode along the East Canal Road, her skirt billowing in the wind, exposing her muscular legs. The jackfruit and guava trees looked washed after the rain. The sun shone on the emerald green lawns of the whitewashed bungalows. The wind blew her hair around his cheeks as she negotiated the winding road until they reached a modest bungalow with a small garden. Her brother sat in a chair wearing a crisp white shirt and a scarf neatly folded around his neck. His blue blazer was slung at the back of his chair, and with his dark glasses and fine features, he almost looked like a movie star.

'Aaha, it is my sister,' he said, not knowing who was with her.

'This is Arun, from the hospital, whom I told you about,' she said, taking his hand as he stood up.

'Is it Dr Arun?' he said, extending his hand.

'Yes, I am. You can call me Arun.'

The smell of food wafted on the warm breeze into the garden through the front door. The curtains swayed gently in the breeze. In the living room hung the garlanded portrait of her father in an Air Force uniform and an oil wick burned with a glow on the ledge beneath the portrait.

Sujata had told Arun a little about her father, whose plane had disappeared during the war with China in 1962. Neither the plane nor the body was ever found. Her mother believed he was still alive somewhere, and that one fine day, he would return through the same door from which he had said goodbye to her. The flame had burned under his portrait ever since his disappearance.

Sujata's mother had not performed any last rites or religious ceremonies, and neither did she go to the Headquarters for his award ceremony. She shunned military wives, or any kind of support. Sujata dreaded the autumn months, because it was in October, around Diwali, that her father had failed to return to the base after dropping off some supplies at the border. At this time of the year, her mother became irrational and somewhat manic. Last year, she had wandered into the bazaar wearing only a flimsy nightgown.

Arun was not sure if her mother was expecting him, and

when she suddenly appeared in the doorway, she seemed more surprised than Arun. She was tall with aquamarine eyes, and skin so pale that it glistened like opaque, off-white marble.

'For a moment I thought it was Major...' she stopped as soon as she saw Arun.

'Come on, Mother, this is Arun from Delhi,' squealed Sujata with some displeasure.

'What took you so long?'

'I told you, I was going to see *Dr Zhivago*.'

'Hello, Arun beta, you are just in time for dinner,' said her mother after a brief visual appraisal of Arun, whose heart was now racing. 'Did you also see the movie?'

'Yes, Aunty. It was very long.'

'Did you like the movie?'

'I liked the music more than the story, but Sujata, I think, liked the story.'

'Was there a lot of song and dance?'

'Mother,' interjected Sujata, 'it is an English movie.'

Her mother opened the cupboard, letting free the old air of wood polish as she took out some fine bone china plates and began to lay the table meticulously, whilst Vinod sat at the table wiggling his fingers as if he was playing an invisible piano.

Sujata's mother caught Arun staring at her husband's portrait. She lowered her eyes, and in a soft voice asked Arun: 'So, where is your family?'

'In England.'

'I thought you were from Delhi.'

'My family immigrated to England a couple of years ago, and I stayed behind to complete my medical training.'

'Oh,' she said, carefully folding a napkin, 'we have never thought of living abroad even though my brother lives in America. Sujata loves Dehradun, don't you dear?'

'Yes, I do mother.' Sujata said with a sardonic nod, as she played with Vinod's hair. She asked Vinod if he would like Arun to read him a story by Ruskin Bond before dinner.

'Tell me about the film first, a story would be nice after dinner, I think.'

Sujata began to narrate the story frame by frame, which would have made David Lean proud. Her mother, as she went about serving the dinner, also seemed engrossed in the details and the nuances of love as she listened to her daughter's narrative. Arun wondered how he could inveigle Sujata to end the story and bring out the book by Mr Bond.

'And then, he is sitting in a tram and he sees Lara pass by, and for a moment he is not sure it is her. Then he recognizes her familiar stride and gets up from his seat in the crowded tram. She crosses the street, and he loses her. He gets off the tram and runs after her, clutches his chest and falls to the ground... Mother, did I hear you sniffle? And then he is surrounded by people on the street as he dies of a heart attack.'

'Was he as handsome as Major Dhillon?' asked Vinod.

'Oh, shut up, Vinod.'

Arun felt a Zhivagoesque pang in his chest on hearing the strange name. The silence was broken by another stifled sniffle from her mother.

After dinner, Arun read the 'The Eyes Have It.' Vinod listened intently and put a finger on his lips every time his mother clattered the plates while clearing the table.

'What a lovely ending, Dr Arun. I hope you will come again to read to me.'

'I would be delighted to read to you again.'

Arun walked back to the hospital as Sujata's mother did not want her to drive after dark. The policemen were everywhere at this time of the night, putting up road blocks with makeshift barriers of oil drums. He avoided a knot of policemen, their cigarette ends glowing in the dark. He dashed into a side alley only to be confronted by a pack of stray dogs. It had been a strange but pleasant evening. He was not sure if he was on the threshold of entering into the realm of Sujata's family or if he would just remember this evening with tender nostalgia for the rest of his life.

When he reached his lodging and opened the door, a brown envelope lay on the floor. He quickly opened it and read: *I am pleased to inform you that the Bishop of Nagpur has approved your stay at the mission for a year.*

He read it again before he went to the next line.

I am afraid the monthly rent will be Rs 200.

That would leave only one hundred rupees to live on. He lay on his unmade bed and fell asleep in his clothes.

❖

Had it not been for the insolence of his fellow intern, Rana, Arun might have been another bystander learning no surgical skills on the surgical rotation with Dr Mishra, who had been busy operating all night. There was a young girl with a burst appendix; a young farmer who had been stabbed, lacerating his kidney; and an old man with gangrenous intestines.

Rana was going through the charts nervously before the rounds. Arun was talking to the patients before the arrival of Dr Mishra, who would usually be in a bad temper after a gruelling spell of night surgery. And this morning, not only did Dr Mishra have the displeasure of meeting the Superintendent but he had also forgotten to pay his son's school fees at the Catholic school. They were a stickler for having the fees paid on time.

With his streaky moustache, Dr Mishra might have looked daunting, but his mouth was always full of betel juice and the bulge of his upper lip made him look like the powerful yet benevolent Hanuman. He walked to the patients who were still groggy from the anaesthesia. The young man who had been stabbed had a resigned look and sat facing the head-end of the bed. He came from the Jaunsar area, where polyandry is still practiced to some extent in the villages. They claim to be the descendants of Queen Draupadi, who in the epic *Mahabharat* was shared amongst the five Pandava brothers. Dr Mishra did not look at the patient or address Arun. He wiggled the plastic tube sticking from a patient's back, draining the blood-tinged fluid into a bag as if he was admiring a piece of art. Then he turned to Rana, who he suspected had gotten into medical school on some quota. Everyone seemed to be getting into medical school under some quota or the other these days: the defence quota, the backward class quota, the freedom-fighter family quota, and, of course, for those who could afford it, the donation quota.

'Rana, aren't you from the Jaunsar district, er, the polyandry area?' asked Dr Mishra. Rana's face reddened instantly and he began to adjust his glasses. 'No, Sir, I am not from Jaunsar,' he said, clearing his throat.

'Where are you from?'

'From Bawar.'

'Well, it is close enough. This man is from Jaunsar. He has a horseshoe kidney. I trust you know what a horseshoe kidney is?'

'Yes, Sir, the two kidneys are joined together.'

'Very good, Rana. Horseshoe is for good luck, usually. Why is it bad luck to have a horseshoe kidney?'

Rana looked a little puzzled, unable to connect why horseshoes should have anything to do with luck. He stood silently, still unable to understand his boss's reasoning. Dr Mishra turned to Arun, raising his eyebrows inquisitively.

'Sir, they are predisposed to kidney stones and infections,' answered Arun.

Rana, of course, was not afraid of Dr Mishra. He was a member of the youth wing of Mrs Gandhi's Congress Party. He spoke at the rallies at Parade Ground in favour of sterilizations as a way to save the country from population explosion. He was a fiery speaker, who rose quickly in the ranks of the political party, and it was rumoured that he was going to sit beside Sanjay Gandhi, the Prime Minister's son, on the podium in the upcoming rally.

As they moved to the next patient, Dr Mishra remembered his son's school fees. 'Rana, you live near Rajpur Road, don't you? Do me a favour, take these three hundred rupees and deposit them in the Catholic school. You can take the afternoon off.'

Rana's face dropped quickly, like a snapped clothes line. In a quiet voice he said, 'Sir, I don't know why I am being asked to do this. I thought I had come here to learn surgery.'

Dr Mishra shifted the betel nuts to the other side of his cheek. He rested his arm on Rana's shoulder and said, 'You have a lot to learn, not only surgery.' Dr Mishra asked Arun if he could deliver the money to the school before 3 p.m. Arun was more than glad to get away from the hospital. As he was leaving, Dr Mishra said, 'Arun, see me in the operating room to assist with the surgeries. Rana, you don't have to attend my rounds anymore.'

❖

The bus was moving at a crawl. The engine had a sonorous drone and the passengers were in a collective reverie. The driver rested his elbows on the steering wheel at the traffic light, waiting for the green signal, and he appeared to be almost dozing off. Arun looked at the meandering traffic ahead. The school was still a mile away and soon it would be three o'clock. It would be quicker to run there.

He dashed to the back of the bus and got off. A policeman in a khaki uniform appeared out of nowhere and cracked his baton on Arun's legs, making him kneel on the road. There was another crack on his back, and he lay on the floor surrounded by many pairs of shoes. The traffic began to move.

The policeman in shorts caught him by the collar and said, 'You donkey, don't you know it is a crime to get off the bus at the traffic light, haan?'

'Yes I know, I know, but I am in a hurry, Officer Sahib.'

'In a hurry, ha ha, everyone is in a hurry son.' He took out a notebook to scribble something and thrust the paper at Arun.

'Pay Rs 30 fine.'

'I don't have any money,' pleaded Arun.

'No money? Let me search you.' He thrust his hands into Arun's pockets and found the notes Dr Mishra had given him. Two or three other policemen appeared when they saw the wad of notes. 'He says he has no money.' They laughed.

'That money does not belong to me, please, Inspector.'

'Arre beta, don't worry. Today the government will give you money. Take him to the vasectomy tent,' commanded the first policeman. Arun's protests were drowned in their guttural laughter, and then one of them kicked him on the head, and he passed out.

The policemen were short of their target quota for sterilization; it was either vasectomies or a cut in the pay cheque. When Arun finally regained consciousness, he could see, across the street, a white tent with a red cross painted on it. Policemen sat on benches outside the tent, smoking cigarettes. They had rounded up some young labourers—who loitered near the Clock Tower looking for work in the local quarry—for minor misdemeanours. Their bodies were covered with white ash from the quarry, which made them look like aliens. An old man came out of the tent, clutching his crotch with one hand and a transistor radio—a gift from the government after the procedure—in the other. He was followed by the men from the quarry, each holding a transistor radio.

Arun's body, still limp from the blow, was carried by two policemen who laid him on the wooden table inside the tent. The voices of the policemen became audible to Arun again, and he groaned as one of them unzipped his trousers. Arun leapt from the table and shouted, 'You bastards, let me go!'

The other policemen held his shoulders and legs. The paramedic, whose back was turned to him, was arranging the surgical tray.

Arun shouted, 'I am a doctor!'

The paramedic turned around, and his face lit with surprise. 'Arre, this is our Doctor Sahib from the hospital.'

The policemen suddenly let go of him and looked at each other, shaking their heads. 'Mishtake, mishtake,' said one of them in his Bihari accent. 'Sahib, why didn't you tell us earlier? Please take a transistor anyway, or take two if you like.'

Arun dusted his clothes, zipped his trousers, grabbed the money from the policeman and ran like a mad man to the Catholic school.

4

The isolation room was small, almost like a cubicle. There was barely any sunlight, except in late autumn when the low sun sent its beams of light into the dark and damp corners, illuminating the single white metallic bed. One could hardly discern the flaking paint peeling off the headboard. On the bed lay Bhag Singh, like a caged skylark, one who was used to the expanse and horizons of a mountain-top village.

He lay there consumed by miliary tuberculosis. He was barely thirty years old or perhaps older, for it was difficult to tell the age of a pahari by his looks. He was darker and taller than most paharis. His chalky teeth almost glowed in the dark. With his hair combed back, revealing a prominent forehead with serene features, he appeared to be one who had accepted the vicissitudes of life as part of his Karma.

Arun put on his face mask and prepared to give him his daily dose of Streptomycin. The milky white drug in the syringe smelled of burning rubber. Bhag Singh had been in the room for almost two-and-a-half months, and with each injection he regained some of his strength. If only he hadn't yawned under a peepul tree, the pret would not have entered his body and possessed him—so he believed.

Three years ago the monsoon had been terrible. The terraced fields of barley and corn had dried up; Bhag Singh left his wife, his younger brother and mother on a whim to find work as a labourer in the nearby hill town.

He went to the town across the mountain range where lights glowed and twinkled after sunset. It was a different world from what he had ever known, but what surprised him the most was the sheer number of electrical lamp posts that lit up the town. There was no electricity in his village. After dark he was used to the canopy of stars. Like most paharis from the villages, he ended up as a labourer and a rickshaw-puller in Mussoorie, hauling well-fed Punjabi ladies from Delhi who could not be bothered to walk up and down the Mall Road. Little did Bhag Singh know that he had almost cut his life expectancy by half, as most of the rickshaw pullers died of tuberculosis by the time they reached the age of thirty. The hill men had no immunity to the tuberculosis bacillus, and with a single contact the bacillus thrived in their lush lungs until there was no room for them to grow; suffocated by sheer numbers, they escaped with a cough to seek new lungs, or risk dying with their host. His lungs looked like moth-eaten fabric.

Bhag Singh stirred in his bed without much fervour. He was used to the arrows of fate loaded with disappointments. Before he could ask about the date of his release from the hospital, Arun lifted his hand and showed two fingers, 'Two more weeks, my friend,' he said and handed the empty syringe to Trishna, who stood behind him. Her eyes sparkled and narrowed above her mask, and Arun felt she was hiding a mischievous smile.

Arun got out of the room as soon as he could. He took off the mask to inhale the fresh air. 'Why were you smiling in there?' he asked Trishna, who was busy settling her hair.

'Did you know,' she said with a giggle, 'Bhag Singh's son was born eighteen months after he left his village.'

'So?' he said, cocking his head.

'Do you know what he said to me when I asked him how this happened?'

'What?'

'"It is god's gift," he said.'

'You believe in god, don't you?"

'Of course, I do. I go to Topkeshwar Temple every Monday and also keep a fast.'

'To get a good husband?'

'Yes, but not a doctor.'

It was almost lunch time. The hospital driveway was full of people, and an army jeep pulled in. The driver in a smart military uniform and a cap sat upright, almost like a statue. The passenger was obviously an officer, a Sikh. His uniform had shiny emblems and ribbons across his upper pocket. He was tall and fair. Sujata emerged from the ER wing with a radiant smile and weaved her way through the crowd towards the jeep.

When Arun saw them, his heart seemed to come up into his throat. A cool gust of wind stung his eyes, and he almost lost his focus as she hopped on to the jeep. In a flash she was gone, and as in the silent movies, he could see them both but was unable to hear. And he almost forgot Trishna was standing close to him.

'That was Major Dhillon,' she said with a smile.

'Well, Sujata does not have to fast to get her man,' said Arun wryly.

❖

That morning, Arun had remembered it was Sujata's birthday. He did not know what to give her. The morning air was still damp and heavy with silvery mist, which shrouded the rose bushes in the small hospital garden. He plucked a fresh rose and put it in the leather case of his portable blood pressure machine. He had hoped to meet Sujata in the emergency room, but she was busy seeing patients and doing minor surgical procedures. There were rounds to be done on the medical floor, intravenous antibiotics had to be infused and patients had to be prepared for surgery on the following day. It was not a day he wanted to be in the hospital. Somehow Trishna sensed this.

'Have you ever been to Kalsi?' she asked him.

'No, never.'

'There is a beautiful canal where you can ride a bicycle to the rock edifice of King Ashoka from the third century.'

'Sounds good. Maybe we can ride there after the rounds.' Arun's mind wandered to the officers' mess. He imagined Sujata being served by uniformed waiters at the bar, and later Major Dhillon carrying her to his bedroom. He missed the vein as he jabbed the patient, and when he tried again, the vein collapsed and oozed blood. He felt frustrated because he had mastered the art of putting in intravenous lines.

'Not having very good luck, I see, Dr Arun.' It was Sujata who suddenly appeared, her face a little flushed.

'No, I am not,' he said without looking at her.

'Let me help you.' Sujata leaned towards him, brushing her forearm against his. She grabbed the needle and gently threaded it into the vein in one stroke. Arun could smell the fragrance of her frizzy hair, which always made her look as though she had just got out of the shower.

'Hey, did you forget something?' she asked him, poking her finger into his ribs.

'No, I didn't. But someone else also remembered your birthday.'

'Hmm, where is my card?'

'Well, I had something special for you.'

'Oh, really?'

From the corner of his eye, he could see Trishna observing them intently while filling the paperwork for the upcoming surgeries. It was late afternoon, and her shift was going to end soon. Arun looked at the leather case of the sphygmomanometer.

'Let me show you,' he said, and walked to the treatment room. He opened the leather case slowly, but to his surprise he did not see the dew-covered red rose, instead there was a twig with withered petals, almost like purple jelly. He quickly zipped back the leather case.

'What is it?' she asked as she pressed close to him.

'It was a rose this morning, but is no more.'

'It is the thought that counts, silly,' she said, as she gave him a fleeting kiss on his cheek. He did not have the courage to ask her where she had been that morning.

'Vinod and my mum have planned something. So long, see you tomorrow,' she said, as she ran down the corridor in her tight white bell bottoms. She gave a robust kick to start her scooter, sat on the seat and gave a push to lift the scooter off the stand. Arun watched her as she disappeared into the traffic.

Trishna came into the treatment room, pretending to look for a saline bottle. 'I hope I did not disturb anything.'

'What do you mean?' asked Arun.

'Well, I don't want to question your judgment Dr Arun. Sujata is full of life, you know what I mean,' she said, as she reached up to the top shelf. She was on her toes, her midriff curving to reveal the sweep of her hips. 'I shouldn't be saying this. It is none of my business.' As she turned around, Arun asked her if she was still interested in cycling to Kalsi after her shift.

After Trishna changed into her regular clothes, she seemed somewhat smaller. Perhaps it was the nurse's cap that made her look tall. She had put on eyeliner, and her dark brown eyes shone like amber in the sunlight. For a moment he imagined her in her wedding sari, her hair in a bun festooned with jasmine flowers and her skin smelling of sandalwood and spices.

He was alone in the treatment room again. Surreptitiously, he opened the leather case again to see the remains of the rose, but strangely the fragrance was stronger.

'What are you thinking about?' asked Trishna.

'Of you!'

'Oh, really? What about me?' inquired Trishna.

'Actually, I was thinking of what Bhag Singh said: It is God's gift!'

'Do you think he will live to see his son?'

'I hope so.'

The bus to Kalsi started from the Clock Tower. It weaved its way through the chaotic bazaar. In the heat of the afternoon, shopkeepers swatted the flies indolently as they watched the slow-moving traffic of tempos, bullock carts overloaded with rice sacks, buses that seemed to be running on one cylinder, and military vehicles with young recruits sweating under tarpaulin tops. As the city receded, the road meandered through small embankments to the open land of the valley, garlanded with shimmering hills.

'This is not like my green Kerala,' Trishna said.

The bus dropped them off at Dak Pathar on the bank of the Yamuna. Here the water-logged rice fields were lush green, reflecting the sun like the thousand pieces of a broken mirror. Here and there white egrets stood patiently, balanced perfectly on one leg. A tube well somewhere in the distance, with its constant rhythm, violated the pure stillness. The air off the river bank, strewn with rounded grey stones, was cool.

Arun suddenly felt liberated. There was inner elation at just being in the presence of another soul on a deserted road.

Trishna hopped on the low embankment wall and stood close to Arun. He held her hand to steady her on the rocks along the embankment of the river. In the distance, on the opposite side of the river, the white domes of the Paonta Sahib gurudwara shimmered in hazy sunlight of the early evening. A flock of low-flying geese flew over the river and disappeared into the mist downstream. Trishna turned her face towards Arun and said: 'Isn't this place so beautiful?'

'So are you,' he said, pulling her towards him. She was facing the setting sun. The cool breeze swept her hair onto her glowing cheeks. He gently brushed the hair away with his fingers. They kissed each other until they fell into a tight embrace on the sand between the smooth gray boulders. Her fragrance lingered on his face, his tongue, his hands. He rested his head on her chest, exhausted.

'I hear you are living in some European compound with an English woman,' she said suddenly.

'Yes, her name is Victoria.'

'Maybe I can visit you there.'

'Sure.'

5

John, the Indian Christian cook, walked from the kitchen to the lawn surrounding the colonial bungalow, carrying the breakfast tray like an English butler. It took him at least five minutes to reach the table covered with a white satin cloth. He did not spill a drop of milk or the tea, which was in a silver-plated kettle. On the tray, he also had crushed ice in a bowl, with freshly peeled litchis placed on top of the ice. A blood-red grapefruit, geometrically sliced inside the peel with a layer of golden-brown honey, attracted the attention of a passing bee, but John was undeterred. He carefully lowered the tray on the table, where Victoria sat as she had done every morning for the past fifteen years after leaving her home on the Isle of Anglesey in North Wales.

Across the lawn stood an ancient peepul tree with heart-shaped leaves through which there was a murmur of the morning breeze. Behind the tree stood a two-storey apartment complex, which remained empty except for the few weeks in a year when it was used by missionaries from overseas.

Victoria lowered her head and clasped her hands in prayer to thank the Lord for His presence. She was thankful for the food on the table, and for the Lord's guidance about subletting the apartment to a young, non-Christian man. John stood behind her until she had finished saying Grace. Then with measured gestures, he carefully unfolded the napkin on her lap.

She wondered what she would do without him in a year's time when she would return to Britain after fifteen years of missionary service in India. She had stumbled upon him quite by chance on a bus trip from Delhi, but she believed it was the Lord's wish…like everything else in her life. It was the Lord's will that John missed the train to Dehradun and sat next to her in the bus. She remembered the line from Ecclesiastes 9:11: '…time and chance happeneth to them all.'

When John had lit a bidi to smoke, Victoria shifted uneasily in her seat. She was the only European on the bus. He was taken aback when she turned to him and admonished him in perfect Hindi, 'Yeh aap ke saheyet ke liye acha nahin.' She had used the word 'aap' for 'you'. He was used to 'tum', less respectful, which the Swiss ambassador's wife, for whom he worked as a cook, used when she addressed him.

He took an instant liking to Victoria and promptly threw the bidi out of the window. During the five-hour journey, John told her how he had learned to cook European food and Swiss desserts at the embassy, and the ambassador's wife had learned Indian cooking from him. But he was tired of Delhi and longed to be near his family in Dehradun.

He never went back to Delhi, and had stayed with Victoria ever since that bus journey. He cooked Indian food for lunch, and dinner was always European fare with a dessert. He knew which vegetables upset her delicate stomach, the lentils she liked and the salads that cooled her during the hot summers. He varied the food according to the seasons and her moods. When she seemed unhappy or lonely, he made Swiss desserts covered with chocolate and fresh cream. He was so familiar with her disposition that, at times, she felt he could almost read her mind; so she was not at all surprised when he asked: 'When is the Doctor Sahib moving in?'

'At the end of the week,' she said nonchalantly.

No. This was not the morning to tell him. The burden weighed heavily upon her heart, and in her Bible reading that morning she turned to Psalms to draw courage to tell him that this was going to be her last year in India. Maybe he already knew, for lately he had been making Swiss chocolate cakes and pastries garnished with fresh pineapple and ornate sugar icings. She noticed he had become rather stoic and incessantly smoked bidis with the most acrid of smells, a habit she detested. He had lost weight, and his trousers hung on his waist as if strung on a clothes' line. Now in his early forties, not much older than her, with his wavy oily hair combed backwards, he almost looked distinguished.

She was startled by the school bell. The leisurely breakfast had made her lose track of time; each morning, she seemed to linger over her breakfast as if it were her last. It was a short walk to the Christian girls' school that housed mostly orphans. She had worked very hard to get government approval to convert it from a middle school to a high school.

She thought of the hours she had spent in dusty government offices, the sweaty paan-chewing officials who eventually gave in to her persistence, but also brought her into the spotlight of the Hindu nationalist party supporters. One official even had the audacity to tell her to leave the country and stop converting poor people to Christianity. But she knew the Lord worked in mysterious ways, and in His name, she worked and prayed for her girls and had the comfort that He would not forsake them. Then Mrs Indira Gandhi declared Emergency, which put an end to the threatening notes at the school's doorsteps.

She turned to John and asked if the postman had come.

'Yes, Miss Sahib,' he said, as he methodically cleared the table. He brought in the letters, and there were several in blue envelopes with airmail stamped across. But the one that demanded attention was a large brown envelope of recycled paper with the government seal of the three lions of Ashoka. She quickly opened it with the butter knife. It was from the Ministry of External Affairs, informing all foreigners to register with the local police station, otherwise their visas would be revoked.

She felt the moisture building up on her upper eyelids. It was the most peculiar area of her body that instantly beaded with sweat when she was fearful. She remembered her sweaty eyelids for the first time when, at the age of four, London was bombed in 1944. The three-storey row house had collapsed around her, immediately killing her mother. She had emerged from the dust and broken slate roof tiles smouldering in blue smoke, almost unscathed. Her Uncle Burt never found his daughter, Jane, who he was playing with at the time. He frantically scoured the rubble with his bare hands, ignoring the marching homeland guards and air-raid sirens warning of another impending attack. That same weekend he put Victoria on a train to North Wales, along with hundreds of other children who were evacuated from London.

When she came of age, her uncle, now Reverend Craig, preaching in a whitewashed Methodist church on a cliff in North Wales overlooking the Irish Sea, implored her to serve the Lord and to show her love of Jesus by serving in an orphanage in India. On a grey and cold morning, she sailed from Southampton to Bombay, via the Suez Canal on a P&O liner called *Chosan*.

She had met Aaron, a young engineer who was off to Australia for a mining job, in the ship's chapel. They had prayed together every evening. She waited for him at mealtimes. He seemed at times to look above her head when talking to her, lost in the infinite possibilities that lay before him over the new horizon. He stood in his white flannels, with his hands on his hips. It was not only the name Arun that reminded her of Aaron, it was also the way Arun stood in his white trousers the first time she saw him.

She opened the blue envelope from Reverend Craig. It read:

Dear Victoria,

I hope you are in good spirits, my child. There are some changes taking place in the Church and elsewhere. We are immensely looking forward to your return at the end of your tenure…

The morning assembly in the girls' school had started. She could hear the girls singing 'Lead kindly light amidst the encircling gloom, lead thou me on.' Mrs DaSouza, the headmistress of the school, had an uncanny habit of choosing hymns that reflected Victoria's moods. She had once told her that this was one of Mahatma Gandhi's favourite hymns.

Victoria called after John. 'I have something very important to tell you,' she said.

'Yes, Miss Sahib,' he said, looking puzzled as she took out her handkerchief to wipe her eyes.

'I will be leaving for England,' she paused, 'forever, in a few months.'

John stood motionless without saying anything. She was surprised at his stoicism. 'England will be very cold,' he said.

'Yes, indeed,' she said with a smile, 'but what will you do when I leave?'

John picked up the tray, and said, 'Miss Sahib, please do not worry about me. I will go back to my village. It is my daughter whom I worry about.'

6

Dr Gupta's husband was in the Superintendent's office, leaning forward in anticipation of seeing Arun, with his hands clasped, his knees perpendicular to the seat. He did not appear to be more than forty. He was in a pinstriped suit and shiny shoes, as if he had just finished arguing a case in the court. The Superintendent stood close to him; when Arun entered the room, she cut her sentence short and simply took a deep breath, which she exhaled in a leisurely fashion with a musical wheeze. After this small sigh she introduced Arun to the lawyer. He did not stand up or shake hands with Arun.

'At last we meet, Dr Arun,' he said, as he extended his long legs and pulled forward his chair without getting up. 'The honourable Superintendent tells me we still have no news of my wife's wedding rings.'

'Unfortunately no, Sir,' said Arun, 'I was witnessing a tragic event and I simply…'

'Now, now, Dr Arun, I have heard that story before. You know, we are not interested in stories, just the whereabouts of the rings. Don't tell me they vanished into thin air.'

Arun looked towards the Superintendent for some support, but she busied herself in polishing her gold-rimmed glasses with a cotton swab dipped in rubbing alcohol. He could not understand her indifference towards him. He felt the arteries in his neck pulsating as he took a deep breath to answer the lawyer.

'Mr Gupta, I don't know if you have ever seen someone die in front of your eyes, someone who was talking to you one minute, and then...fell silent forever. I watched a young girl bleed to death. Yes, your wife did hand her wedding rings to me. And I seem to have lost them. I take full responsibility.'

'Do you know how much they were worth? Perhaps you will never know. The diamonds in those rings belonged to my great-great-grandmother. Those diamonds had been on the fingers of three generations of my family. Either you find them or risk not getting your completion certificate from the gracious Superintendent of the hospital. Correct me if I am wrong, Superintendent Madam.'

She did not answer. As a woman of authority, she knew when to be silent when dealing with men. Although she had no children of her own, she had learned to treat men as children, and silence was an important instrument in her armoury. 'So you have lost them...is that all you can say?' she asked.

'I am terribly sorry, but in that moment of fear, nothing mattered to me. Nothing. I can still see the face of the dying young woman, but I hardly remember what the rings looked like.'

Mr Gupta pulled away his chair towards the window. He stood up facing the window as if in quiet reflection, then putting his hand under his chin, he suddenly turned around facing Arun. 'Young man, have you ever read a short story by Guy de Maupassant, "The Diamond Necklace"?'

'No, Sir.'

'Well, I suppose they don't teach you anything more than Medicine in medical school. In that fascinating story, Madame Loisel loses a diamond necklace and pays a terrible price. You know there is a price for everything. A price for heroism, a price for mistakes, even genuine mistakes. Now, I am a Gupta and also a lawyer. I have been trained to put a price on anything and everything, but I don't want you to pay a terrible price, just something you or your family can live with. I think three thousand rupees is a reasonable sum. Isn't that so, Superintendentji?

She nodded in agreement and cleared her throat. 'We may also have to write an incident report for the record.'

'But Ma'am, three thousand rupees is almost a year's worth of my stipend,' pleaded Arun.

'I have nothing more to add,' she said. 'Please get back to your work.'

Mr Gupta smiled at his accomplishment as he folded the papers on which he'd been taking notes. Beneath his suave veneer, Arun thought, lurked a complex man.

Sujata had been listening to this exchange from the corridor, standing behind the door that was half-ajar. She was always effervescent and talkative, a keeper of all the hospital gossip. She had reasons to believe that Dr Gupta's marriage had taken a shaky path after the loss of the wedding rings.

'So how was your interrogation?' asked Sujata when Arun came out of the room.

'I think I did fine. Mr Gupta wants three thousand rupees for those rings. By the way, have you ever read Guy de Maupassant?'

'Never heard of him.'

'I want to read his short story "The Diamond Necklace". Where do you think we can find it?' asked Arun impatiently, as he tried to keep up with her brisk strides.

'Maybe the local library, or hmm...I have a better idea, at the Doon Club library. But why this sudden enthusiasm for this fellow, Guy...the...what did you say?'

'Well, Mr Gupta mentioned the story. I could read it to Vinod; I have not seen him for a while.'

❖

Sujata avoided going to the Doon Club, which had been frequented by her father before his disappearance. The club was behind the public park with rows of cherry trees. The colonial building with a 'Members Only' sign on the iron gate since the British times was now patronized by service personnel, business owners and bankers, and anyone who considered themselves to be among the elite, or elite enough to don bow ties and suits at the clubhouse fundraisers for the poor.

Victorian crystal chandeliers hung from the mahogany beams on the ceiling. Although dusty from many summers, they still split the light into rainbow colours across the jaded walls, illuminating the sepia-coloured photographs of the sahibs and memsahibs of the 1920s. The bar with smoked glass reflected the vintage whiskey and soda bottles in subdued lighting so as not to distract the players at the pool table. Whilst the men played pool, women in glittering saris played bridge. The library, which had an extensive collection of old books in glass-fronted mahogany cupboards, was the least occupied. Waiters in white turbans and flowing robes carried cocktails named by the British—Poison, Double Major and Pretty Polly.

When Sujata and Arun entered the club, the waiters smiled at her. The club smelled of beer, cigar smoke and the perfumes of yesteryear. Sujata cheerily waved at the group of ladies at the bridge table. She called a waiter. 'Poison for the sahib. He needs it. Cheese dumplings and tea for me.'

'What is Poison, anyway?' asked Arun.

'Oh, it is gin, vodka, and lime juice with a secret ingredient for passion.'

'Well, once I consume this poison, it may make me utter some undisclosed longing.'

She leaned toward him, her elbows on the table with her hands cupping her face. 'Like what?' she said, and burst out laughing. The locket around her neck swung forward.

'Tell me, Sujata, how do you keep so happy? Who gave you this locket?'

She leaned back in her chair, biting her lower lip. Her liquid green eyes welled up with tears. 'My father,' she said. She carefully opened the heart-shaped locket, and revealed a tooth wrapped in cotton wool. 'My father's wisdom tooth. It was very painful for him when it was extracted. I have painted it with clear nail polish to preserve it,' she said. 'I am happy I have something of my father that I can feel.'

'I am so sorry, Sujata, I did not mean to...'

'You asked me how I am always happy. I am happy I got into medical school relatively easily because my father was a war hero. My mother would have killed herself in her bouts of depression had it not been for my blind brother. There is a lot to be thankful for. You know, I used to come here with my father on Sundays.'

'You must have been very young.'

'Yes. Children were allowed into the club only on Sundays.'

Arun drank the 'poison', which indeed lived up to its name, for it tasted like Dettol mixed with lime cordial. He looked towards the window that faced the grounds; it framed the distant Camel's Back in purplish hues of the twilight. Warm yellow lights on top of the mountains seemed to move and shimmer. He did not know if the poison was taking its effect.

Sujata held him by his arm. 'Let's go find this Guy de Maupassant.'

The floor-to-ceiling bookshelves were well stocked. The books smelled of cigar smoke and the dampness of bygone monsoons. Some of the books might well have been first editions, *Doon Valley Flora and Fauna*, *Works of Geological Survey of India*, *The Princely States of India*. And there were the usual classics: William Shakespeare, Charles Dickens, Rudyard Kipling, John Lang and John Masters. They were both surprised to find the complete stories of Maupassant next to *Nightrunners of Bengal* by John Masters. Arun hurriedly turned the cover, and sure enough, there was the story, 'The Diamond Necklace'.

It was dark by the time they left the Doon Club. The only road that was lit was Rajpur Road. It was a circuitous route to her house, but Sujata did not want to drive her scooter on the back roads. Arun had hoped she would, so that he could hold on to her waist in the dark.

She turned her scooter towards Rajpur Road. 'We'd better get some fried fish for Vinod and Mum. They love it,' said Sujata.

There was a caravan of wooden carts by the roadside, each lit with a gas lamp. On display were fresh fillets of river fish marinated in orange-coloured paste and yoghurt mixed with cumin seeds. In the centre of the cart lay a cauldron of boiling mustard oil, sending pungent plumes of smoke into the evening air as the fish-seller dropped the fillets into the oil with aplomb. The fish fillets were sold by the weight; Sujata picked the pieces that were less heavily marinated. Once deep fried, the vendor sprinkled special spices and fresh lemon juice over them.

'Mum, look who is here,' she said, as she took off her helmet.

'Why so late?' inquired her mother.

'Oh, Arun wanted to get a book to read to Vinod. Where is he?'

Vinod came limping out of the kitchen. He had fallen a few days ago, after slipping in the bathroom. 'Is that you, Dr Arun?

'Yes. How is your knee?'

'Much better. Nice to hear your voice again. Are you going to read to me tonight?'

'Yes. I am going to read a short story by a French author, Guy de Maupassant.'

Sujata held Vinod's hand and guided him into a chair. 'Don't hassle Arun too much. He has had a hard day with Dr Gupta's lawyer-husband.'

'Oh, did you resolve the issue?' asked Vinod.

'In a way, yes. I have to come up with three thousand rupees.'

Sujata's mother began to lay the table. It was almost like a ritual, as she meticulously placed the silverware around the quarter plates and full plates. Arun wondered if all the Army wives did the same. After finishing dinner, Sujata's mother asked Arun if he had heard from his family in England.

'Yes, Aunty, my mother writes to me, but she never conveys what is happening. She always writes: "We are fine. I hope you are fine and looking after your health." I can't tell if they are happy in England. Oh, yes, in her last letter she mentioned that at last she had got a job in some sort of a factory.'

'In a factory!' She looked puzzled. She took off her apron and sat in a wicker chair. 'Arun, if your mother had been in India, do you think she would have worked in a factory? I don't know why people go to foreign countries. After your training, you will also go to England. In our own country we need doctors. Do you know that children die from malaria and burst appendices every day here? Majority of your classmates will go to Western countries, which is a shame, really. I will never let Sujata go to a foreign land.'

'Mum, it's because you just want me stay near you. I don't think you even want me to go to Delhi for my house job.'

'No, seriously, Sujata. You were telling me there is a 30 per cent chance of a child born in India reaching the age of five. How many countless women die in childbirth in the villages? It is a shame for our country. And look at those Christian doctors from the West who spend their lives in remote villages. Look at Dr Lehman in Herbertpore, who has restored the sight of hundreds of people. Unfortunately, he couldn't do anything for my Vinod's sight.'

'But, Aunty, we don't have enough training hospitals.'

'Beta, we don't need specialists. We need people for basic care. If you can save someone from dying from dehydration, isn't that something?'

'Story time!' interrupted Vinod, as he hobbled on his injured knee.

Arun blew the dust off the cover of the book. He recounted how Mr Gupta had mentioned the story to him in connection with the loss of his wife's wedding rings. Arun cleared his throat and began to read: '*The girl was one of those pretty and charming young creatures who sometimes are born, as if by a slip of fate, into a family of clerks. She had no dowry, no expectations, no way of being known, understood, loved, married by any rich and distinguished man...*'

At the end of the story, Vinod exclaimed: 'Dr Arun, the solution to the problem is in the story! You don't have to give even a single rupee! Just tell Mr Gupta the diamond rings were fake, otherwise why would his wife have worn priceless diamond rings to work?'

7

A couple of days earlier, Arun had moved into the apartment building across from Victoria's bungalow. The building was used infrequently by visiting missionaries and by Mr Roy, an Indian Christian bachelor who worked for the Health Ministry and came once a year to donate money to her school. The windows had remained unlit until Arun arrived, but now at night, light splashed onto the lawn with a warm glow. She had not seen him since he had arrived with a small suitcase and a bicycle.

She woke up startled and her heart was pounding. She had had a dream which took her more than a decade back to when she had visited Australia to see Aaron after their maiden journey from Britain. She did not know why she had been dreaming about Australia that morning, or Aaron for that matter. The fervour of her youth and unforeseen desires had led her all the way to Australia. It was the kind of dream that slips away from memory the more one tries to recollect it. She rarely dreamed, and Aaron was someone who occupied a ledge in her mind, the path to which was still accessible through the canyons of her memory which she feared to tread. Was it the presence of Arun in the vicinity that made her dream, or was it pure nostalgia for what might have been? It frightened her, and when she opened her eyes, she was glad to be in a cocoon of reality, rather than in the dream of being with Aaron, still young, and not a day older than when she'd first set her eyes upon him on the ship.

She could hear John in the kitchen, making the familiar early morning noises: filling up the kettle and igniting the kerosene stove with the hiss of the lotus-shaped blue flame, to make her morning tea. The wooden beams of the bungalow creaked as the sun warmed up the corrugated tin roof. She felt safe under the mosquito net strung above her bed. She picked up the Bible beside her bed and began to read.

She enjoyed mornings the most. Even John knew it was sacrilege to disturb her with mundane things, so he quietly left the tea tray on the night stand. As she listened to the drip of the frost melting from the roof top and the boisterous claps of the wings of the parrots in the litchi trees, she made a list of things to do.

❖

After two years in India and exchanging letters with Aaron, who had got a mining job in Darwin, Victoria had become restless and wanted to visit Australia. The Bishop of Nagpur, her superior, noticed the urgency in her eyes as she pleaded for a furlough for a few weeks. Reluctantly, he had sanctioned her leave from the orphanage. 'My child,' he said, 'the further you go, the less you know.'

She remembered how Aaron had teased her about Dehradun, that funny sounding name for a sleepy town, which had inspired George Harrison to write a song. Walking on the beach, holding Victoria's hand, he hopscotched as he sang:

Dehra Dun, Dehra Dun, many roads take you there,
Many different ways
Many people on the roads looking at the sights
Many others with their troubles looking for their rights
Dehra Dehra Dun

See them move along the road in search of life divine
Beggars in a goldmine

Victoria wanted to tell him this road, too, did not lead anywhere. She was overwhelmed with homesickness, not for the churches and castles of her native Britain, but for the dirt roads of Dehradun, the chimes of the temples, the hustle and bustle of life around her, the poverty, the squalor, all seemed sacred to her in Australia's sterile landscape. She felt the Bishop was wrong. The further she travelled, the more she knew about herself. Or was the Bishop right about something she did not know?

As the sun set over the Indian Ocean, illuminating wisps of clouds with golden edges, Aaron had said, 'Come to Australia. What are you doing in Dehradun?' He picked up some sand in his hands, 'All the minerals are here to mine, even uranium. What do you seek in India? Only roads that lead nowhere.'

She walked quietly. If only she could tell him how plain she found Australia. There were no twisted roads full of life leading nowhere. There was no squalor or suffering, and how could she know Christ without suffering? She felt the warmth of his hands on her shoulders, but it was his ambition that frightened her. She could not imagine living the rest of her life in Australia, a land so vast, its sky like an inverted bowl that seemed to enclose her spirit in its dome.

After two weeks in Australia, she longed to hear the choir of orphan girls in the morning assembly of her school. Walking along the beach, now bathed in moonlight, she saw a family making a bonfire. It reminded her of the fires she'd seen after the sugarcane harvest in Dehradun. Dotted along the road leading to the valley were small volcano-like furnaces, around which stood farmers silhouetted against the glow, boiling sugarcane juice in giant cauldrons.

But there was no smell of burnt sugar with this bonfire. To her surprise, she heard an Indian accent as one lady said to another: 'Alka, I tell you, my Australian daughter-in-law loved the masala shops in Paltan bazaar and she loves to cook Indian food. Mind you, she uses Madhur Jaffrey's cookbook.'

'Sounds like your Indian friends,' said Aaron as they went past a group of women. She wanted to pull away from Aaron and surprise them by talking in Hindi. Perhaps they were from Dehradun.

The women were standing around a small bonfire against the deepening violaceous dusk. Victoria strode up to them and struck up a conversation. Soon the women were laughing and throwing up their arms and hugging each other around the bonfire. Aaron stood in the distance watching, as if they were performing a pagan ritual.

'Aaron, you wouldn't believe this. These women are from Dehradun.'

All of a sudden Victoria felt at home hearing the cheerful voices of the women. She held Aaron's hand and looked at his face. 'I want to leave for India this week,' she said suddenly.

'You really surprise me. You really do. Australia is a gold mine. Go back to your beggars if you wish.'

'Aaron, I think you misunderstood the song. It is not the Indians who are beggars in a goldmine, it is us.'

If ever there was a stark contrast between two countries, it was Australia and India. Aaron's and her roads had only briefly intersected. She took a flight back to India a week earlier than planned.

After she left Australia, his letters had a touch of formality, and she no longer waited in anticipation for the postman. The letters stopped coming soon after, and so did the dreams. One day had become quite like another. She prayed and taught at the school. She prayed at mealtimes and before going to bed and waking up. Yet, she never felt alone because she was always in the presence of Christ, but she felt lonely.

❖

That morning, she had an appointment to see Pritam Singh. He brought his seven-year-old niece, Gurpreet, who had been orphaned recently, for admission to the school. He said her parents had been killed by militants, as her father was a police officer. Gurpreet survived because she was at school. In the past, Victoria had admitted some children to the school who were supposedly orphans but later she found the parents were alive and well and just wanted the children to be in a better school.

Pritam Singh was tall and wore a bright red turban, and was perhaps in his late forties. His aquiline nose and searing eyes somewhat intimidated Victoria. The little girl with an angelic face and two pigtails sat quietly in a corner. On her right wrist was a delicate steel kara. 'Mr Singh, you do realize we teach about the love of Jesus Christ to our schoolchildren?'

'Madam, I know you will only teach good things to the children. Guru Nanak was a seeker of Truth, and he said Sat Nam, God is Truth. If Isaah Messeh is Truth, I have no problem with that. Then Isaah Messeh will find Gurpreet. My only request is not to take off her kara. It was given to her by her mother.'

Victoria avoided talking about other faiths, and for a moment she reflected on what he had said: Christ will find Gurpreet. In fact, Christ *had* found her.

'She is so pretty. Does Gurpreet mean pretty?' asked Victoria, patting the child.

'No, it means the beloved of Guru,' said Pritam Singh.

She offered some freshly baked ginger biscuits made by John, but Gurpreet was too shy to accept the offering. Victoria had often thought about adopting a child before she left India, but she was anguished over uprooting a child to a strange country. Deep in her heart she hoped Pritam Singh was telling the truth. He seemed an amiable and simple fellow. He worked as a deliveryman for the local gas company. 'Any time you need cooking gas cylinders, Madam, please let me know,' he said.

❖

As she walked back to the bungalow through the fruit orchard, she lifted her white sari above her pale ankles to avoid catching any brambles. The mid-afternoon air was still and heavy with the aroma of the litchi fruits and islands of dried leaves under the avenue of trees. Victoria observed the lights of Arun's room were still on. Perhaps he had left for the hospital in a hurry that morning, or he liked to return to a lighted room after dark.

She looked forward to the game of Scrabble she played once a week with her friend Elizabeth, an English girl from Blackpool. Elizabeth had married an Indian doctor—one of the few who trained in Britain and returned to his homeland to practice medicine. She wanted to tell Elizabeth about her 'new tenant' and the silly dream she had about Aaron. Elizabeth had told her some of her own strange dreams and occasional nightmares, as she tried to adapt to her new country. She liked the English dishes and the Swiss desserts John made for them. She was not particularly a church-going person. In fact, the last time she was in a church was at Blackpool when she got married to Mohan. She laughed every time the pastor pronounced his name as Mo-Haan, as if it were a German name. She was much younger than Victoria and had a divergent view of life, but the two women had a common heritage and could laugh at themselves. Or sometimes at the idiosyncrasies of Indians.

'You know what Mohan did this morning? He added salt to his orange juice! I learn something new every day. But then he hates Marmite because it reminds him of something dreadful.'

'Oh, for heaven's sake,' laughed Victoria.

They settled down to a roasted leg of lamb with mint sauce, one of John's culinary marvels which he had improved upon after his tenure at the Swiss embassy. Victoria said Grace with eyes closed, thanking the Lord for blessing the food she was about to receive. Elizabeth observed her with reverence and said Amen. Victoria told her about her dream about Australia and how youthful Aaron had looked after all these years.

'Do you still think of him?' asked Elizabeth.

'Not really. No, heavens, no. It was just a dream. When your memories visit only as dreams, it is such a blissful feeling.'

'I hear you have a young tenant on the premises.'

'I haven't seen him since he moved in. His lights are on. I think I may have charged him too much rent. I hope the poor fellow has enough money left to eat.'

'Maybe you should check up on him. Why don't you send John to find what's going on?' asked Elizabeth.

'I hope he hasn't been kidnapped or something.'

John agreed to walk to the apartment. He took the roast lamb and covered it with another plate and a chequered cloth, to keep it warm. As he passed the stairs to the apartment, he noticed Arun's bicycle. He became breathless climbing the flight of stairs. He knocked at the door several times but there was no answer. He put the tray on the floor, and as he moved away he heard a strange noise; it was almost as if someone was talking to themself.

He hurried down the stairs and walked to the bungalow, where the two women were engrossed in a game of Scrabble. John's face looked as though he had seen an apparition and alarmed Victoria. She switched off the gramophone, which was playing Greig's 'In the Hall of the Mountain King'. Over the years, Victoria had learned to glean more information from John's facial expressions than his speech, and she knew immediately something was amiss.

'Noise from inside,' he said, trying to catch his breath. 'Door not open.'

'Victoria, do you have a spare key?' asked Elizabeth.

'Yes, I do.'

It was getting dark. Victoria picked up the flashlight from her bedroom. They marched to the apartment and knocked on the door. There was no answer. Victoria gingerly turned the key and slowly opened the door. The lights were on in the room. Strewn on top of the bed were jackets, shirts and bathing towels, and somewhere underneath the blankets was Arun, with his arm dangling from the bed. The two women looked at each other and then called his name. He moved.

'Thank god, Victoria, he is alive!' said Elizabeth, as she moved closer and lifted the blanket from his face. He was flushed, and his eyes were glazed and half shut. Victoria put her hand on his forehead, 'He is burning like an oven.'

'Victoria, John can fetch Mohan from the clinic. Don't you worry; everything will be fine. Let's turn him on his side.'

As they tried to turn him, he began to shake and drew up his knees. He was still for a minute, and then he started shivering. Sweat broke out on his forehead almost like a spray. He began to whisper, 'I am sorry. I am very, very cold.' He began to shiver again.

It did not take very long for Dr Mohan to drive to the compound in his Morris Minor. He walked into the room, kissed his wife on the cheek, and then gave Victoria a hug.

'Now, what do we have here?' He carefully checked the pulse and observed Arun as he had another bout of shivering. 'A simple case of malaria, but he is very dehydrated. He will need to go to the hospital as a patient, I am afraid.'

8

Like a restless winged insect suspended in a spider's web on a rainy day, hoping for a gust of wind to free him, Arun lay on the metal hospital bed connected to an intravenous infusion. The soles of his feet were burning like hot coals as the wave of fever swept over him. He knew he was drenched in sweat. Too weak to wipe his brow, he muttered to himself as he tried to make sense of the flashes of delirium that flickered like sheet lightning illuminating a bleak landscape. And then he could think again.

Aware of the weight of every muscle of his body, he began to shiver. The word malaria raced in his memory, and he tried to recall the life cycle of the parasite. Merozytes, millions of them rushing in his blood stream. Hypnozytes hiding in his liver. Schizonts, like silos full of merozytes, tearing his red blood cells to pieces. He stared at the ceiling which had water marks like cumulous clouds. He heard voices:

'Madam, he will be fine in a day or two; malaria, you know, is quite common here.'

'I thought he was dying.'

'Well, malaria can kill if left untreated. How do you know Dr Arun, if I may ask?'

'Oh, he is renting a place at the Christian compound.'

'I didn't know he is a Christian.'

'I don't think he is. But I am happy he is in safe hands.'

'Madam, it is the humble cinchona bark extract—chloroquine—which is going to cure him. At least we have plenty of it in the hospital, if nothing else. I shouldn't be saying this... You never know who is listening these days.'

'Thank you, Doctor.'

'Where are you from, if I may ask?'

'I am from the UK.'

'You mean Great Britain. I don't know why they changed the name. It is like calling Queen Elizabeth QE.'

'May I see him before I leave?'

'Sure, staff nurse Trishna will take care of you.'

❖

At the entrance to the hospital, in between the gridiron of the Vespa and Lambretta scooters, a woman in a sari was sweeping up a golden-yellow dust cloud. The town was just coming to life in the morning. A woman sat cross-legged by the roadside blowing furiously, trying to light her makeshift charcoal pit to roast sweet corn. The scooter rickshaws with shrill two-stroke engines spewing blue smoke did not seem to alter the gait of staid cows as they sauntered in between the traffic of humans and bicycles. The bicycle bells rang more for their ringers' pleasure than anything else. The crows in the banyan trees flew in between the branches. Schoolgirls in blue-and-white uniforms took short cuts through the hospital to their school at the opposite end. Everything was in motion.

Trishna, in her crisp white nurse's uniform, avoided the dust cloud as she hurried with Victoria to Arun's room, fanning her nose with her hand. Arun lay curled up in a blanket. His hair had lost its sheen, and his pale face was peppered with facial hair like iron filings.

Only a week ago Victoria hardly knew him, and now she felt somewhat responsible for him. She had prayed for him that morning and, surprisingly, he had constantly been in her thoughts. She wanted to comb his hair into place with her fingers, but it was only a thought. It was Trishna who did exactly what she was thinking, as if she had read Victoria's mind. 'There, Dr Arun, now you look decent for Miss Lambert,' she said as she bent over to put a pillow behind his back. Arun could smell the familiar sandalwood aroma of her skin.

'Thank you for coming to see me.'

'You frightened me. I didn't know whom to contact, or how to get in touch with your folks. I am so glad you are much better.'

'You saved me.'

'It is the Lord who saved you.'

'I think Dr Kumar should be able to release me today.'

Trishna felt she should take charge of the situation. She ordered him to open his mouth. Carefully, she slid the glass thermometer under his tongue. 'Now, listen to me Arun,' said Victoria, 'when you come home, you can have all your meals with me. John won't mind. In fact, he will be happy to cook for us both; he is bored cooking just for me, and don't worry about paying me.'

Trishna pulled out the thermometer from his mouth. '102 degrees Farenheight, down from 104.'

'Thank the Lord,' he found himself saying. 'I don't have some dreadful disease.'

Trishna took his pulse with one hand, and with the other smoothed the crease in the blanket underneath his chin, while her eyes rested on the upside-down intravenous fluid bottle. She also noted that Sujata was standing outside the door, holding a bouquet of flowers, with the other interns. She glided around the small room and kept chatting with Miss Lambert, hoping the crowd outside would disappear.

The young woman was now sweeping the corridor, her hips swaying in the opposite direction of the broom strokes. Sodi adjusted his turban and tilted his head to have a better look. He had a penchant for sweeper girls. They were without make-up and without any pretensions, raw. Trishna avoided Sodi as much as she could because he was known for his lascivious stares, but what irked her more this time was Sujata with those flowers.

Rana did not like Sodi either, and he caught Sodi staring at the young sweeper woman. 'Why don't you go after women of your social standing, after all you are the son of a Colonel, I believe?' Rana asked Sodi with a disdainful curve of his mouth.

'Arre, I keep my fundamentals clear. I keep everything simple, Rana. You only know what you learned in medical school,' said Sodi, patting Rana's back.

As soon as Victoria left the room, the interns entered. Trishna wore a frown as she busied herself with filling the nurse's forms. Sujata happily breezed in with a stethoscope around her neck. 'Where did you disappear to, Mr Arun? Why couldn't you choose a more exciting illness?' asked Sujata.

Rana took off his thick glasses. He looked more bewildered than usual, his eyes larger without the glasses. He spoke in pure Hindi, 'I have been working extra nights for you. Dr Mishra, you know, hates me and gave me, just me...' he looked at Sujata and Sodi, 'all the extra work. But I will settle my account with him one day. Through my political connections, I will have him transferred to some... some godforsaken place in Bihar.'

Sujata and Sodi looked at Rana with amusement, not sure if he wanted Trishna to hear this, for surely his remarks would get to Dr Mishra's ears. Sodi, whose eyes were still following the graceful movements of the sweeper woman in the corridor, turned to Rana: 'You will neither make a good politician nor a good doctor. But one thing I know, you will be the first one to land a job.'

Arun thanked them for coming to see him. The chloroquine was making him nauseated, almost like an incoming tide, a little stronger each time. He turned to his side and felt as if his stomach had fallen down a steep waterfall. He wanted desperately to breathe the air, and gave a deep heave with all the strength he could muster to keep his head above the water. There was another wave of nausea, a churning, a fullness, and then the embankment gave way. He vomited. Trishna grabbed a towel and asked everyone to leave.

'Arun, please get well soon. Vinod is waiting for you to read him another story,' Sujata said.

'Please close the door after you,' said Trishna. She unbuttoned his shirt and wiped his chest gently, and he felt the coolness of her soft hands. Then she picked up the flowers beside his bed and promptly threw them into the trash can along with the dirty towel. 'She could have brought you something decent, instead of these silly flowers.'

9

If ever there was a courtyard in paradise, it was here. The bungalow stood on a square of green. At some distance from the bungalow was a banyan tree, with its brooding branches touching the ground. On one side was a grove of litchi trees that led to the unpaved driveway. Surrounding the other side was a forest of sal and eucalyptus trees that whispered whenever the breeze swept down the mountains.

John had set up the breakfast table on the porch in front of the bungalow, facing the banyan tree. The silverware glinted in the morning sun. Arun was used to eating alone, mostly at cheap restaurants and wayside stalls, and the thought of having formal meals with an English lady somewhat daunted him.

He looked at his fingernails; they seemed clean enough and clipped. Victoria seated herself opposite him. Her white satin blouse gave a glow to her milky white forearms. He carefully unfolded the napkin, which seemed ironed. There was a bowl of fresh strawberries cut into halves like little hearts and litchis on cubes of ice. Arun picked up the fork to pierce the strawberries.

Before he could take the fruit to his mouth, Victoria put her elbows on the table and clasped her hands, 'Shall we say Grace?' She closed her eyes, lowering long blond eyelashes. 'Our father, who art in heaven, give us this day, our daily bread....Amen.'

'Amen,' he said. His face blushed long enough like an uncontrollable yawn as he picked up the fork again. What a beautiful line, he thought: Give us this day. A request to God to grant us forgiveness, deliverance from evil, and fullness of living. Why was there no such ritual in his Hindu household? The Muslims say Bismillah before meals, the Christians say Grace, but in his household the food was taken for granted, and usually his grandmother or mother would have to call two or three times—the food is ready—before anyone would show up.

One ritual his grandmother always performed was to salute the sun the first thing in the morning. She also watered the holy tulsi plant in the courtyard, which was the sunniest part of the house. Without the Sun devta, his grandmother had told him, there would be no food or life on earth. In a way, she gave thanks for the food before she received it, a prayer in anticipation rather than deliverance. An economy in prayers for the day.

John brought white toasted bread cut into perfect triangles. 'I hope you are feeling strong enough to go to work?' she asked.

'I am. But I am not looking forward to the assignment in the leper colony in Dalanwala.'

'Why not?'

'I feel depressed when I see human beings...sort of minimized of their former selves.'

'Physically they may be minimized, as you say, but their spirits are not. I hope you will have a blessed day. An interesting day, I hope,' she said, as she picked a chilled litchi with a tiny fork. She thought about Lazarus and the compassion of Christ. She felt His presence everywhere, not only on this beautiful morning but also on the gloomiest of days and in the dreariest of places. If only Arun could experience His compassion, His presence even in the leper colony...

❖

The bus ride ended a mile away from the edge of the forest of sal trees. The road curved around the hill to reveal single-storey dwellings clinging to the slopes of the hills. It was a gentle climb on foot towards the colony. The Himalayan langoors swung around the sal trees with abandon.

It was not a conglomerate of people as the word 'colony' suggested; instead, it appeared to be a mediaeval hamlet where people seemed to be going about their daily chores. Women were gathering wood, and men were watering a garden patch, some children were playing in the sunlight, their laughter echoing in the hills. From a distance the adults looked normal until one came closer, then the saddled noses and missing digits became apparent. Near the arched stone-entrance to the colony, stood a young man of Arun's age in front of an easel, with a paint brush stuck between his teeth.

Arun noticed all his fingers were missing. 'You are a good painter,' said Arun, trying to catch his breath.

'And who are you?' he replied without looking at him.

'I have come to see you from the hospital.'

'Do you see the colour of my hair? It has turned golden-brown. And there are these white patches on my arms and legs ever since the doctor started me on this new medicine. Methi tells me soon I will become a white man.'

'Who is Methi?'

'She is a girl from Punjab who lives here. I call her Methi because she loves to eat methi. She is also a good painter.' Turning towards the canvas, he began to paint a bougainvillea bush with the brush in between his teeth.

'Where are you from?'

He moved his head in rapid movements as he painted.

He placed the paint brush on a ledge, and looking towards the horizon, said: 'From very, very far away...Cochin.'

'What is your name?'

'Raman.'

'How did you get here?'

'Do you really want to know?'

'Yes, tell me your story.'

'You must first help me light my cigarette. Methi usually lights it for me.' There was a gap in the stone wall where the end of a cigarette was sticking out. He pointed toward his pocket. Arun took out the matchbox and lit the cigarette. 'Smoking is not good for you.'

'When you have a disease as dreadful as leprosy, you should not care about small diseases. I was fourteen years old when I noticed something was wrong with me. One day, when I was playing football at school, I could not kick the ball. My foot became too heavy for me, it became numb and I began to limp.' He leaned towards the wall to pick up the cigarette with his lips, and inhaled deeply, and then, like a blow dart, he deposited the cigarette in the stone alcove.

'At first, my father, who worked in the village post office, thought it was a sprain and tried various Ayurvedic medicines, but then I started developing ulcers that would not heal. I became clumsy with my hands and had difficulty writing. One day, my father said: "Raman, I am taking you to Trivandrum," and there they diagnosed me with leprosy. My father was afraid to take me back to the village because leprosy was unheard of among Brahmins. He was afraid to touch me, and he made me promise not to tell anyone. He was afraid my sister would not get married if anyone in the Brahmin community got a whiff of my diagnosis before the wedding. Brother, the longest bus ride of my life was from Trivandrum to Cochin. I cried and cried all the way, but when I got home, there was no sadness left in me. My uncle, who was visiting from the Middle East, had heard about this place in the North, far away from Cochin, where I could be treated.'

'Do you feel sad now?'

'I feel sad for my mother. Of course, everyone thinks I am working with my uncle in the Middle East. I used to wear clothes like you, and now I feel imprisoned by my disease and wear this white uniform.'

'Will you introduce me to Methi?'

'Yes, of course. But you must also meet Dada.'

'Who is Dada?'

'Dada,' he chuckled, 'is like my grandfather, my mentor. He is one of the oldest leprosy patients here. He was a professor in Bengal, a very learned man. He wants me to marry Methi even though we don't speak the same language. You know what he said to me when I told him I felt imprisoned by my disease? He said: "Son, every human being carries some private prison in his heart."'

Arun walked with Raman to the clinic, where some mothers were waiting with their young children. The place looked surprisingly clean, with neat little flowerbeds full of gladioli. The row of ranchers on the brow of the hill reminded him of deserted military barracks. Outside the clinic was a flagpost without a flag. Leaning against the flagpost, sat an old man with a sparse beard and no eyebrows. His shiny chocolate brown skin glowed in the sunlight. The colony seemed as peaceful as any Shangrila.

'I presume this is Dada,' asked Arun.

'Yes,' said Raman. Arun joined his hands to greet him.

'I will be coming to see you for the next few weeks.'

The old man nodded and said, 'Welcome.'

'You must have lived here for a long time.'

'Yes,' Dada paused. 'But it does not seem long.'

❖

That evening when Arun returned to the bungalow, he found Victoria was not in. On the mantelpiece was a note:

Arun, I will be back at 8 p.m. after the church meeting. The food is in the fridge. If you are free later we can play a game of Scrabble.

On the wall was a portrait of Jesus on the cross, and on the mantelpiece were two bone china plates, one showing the House of Commons and the other a rural scene with a thatched cottage on rolling hills somewhere in England. On the mahogany table lay the Scrabble board with only one tray of letters, but scribbled on the sheet were two scores in the same handwriting with bold strokes. Arun wondered if Victoria had been playing the game with herself.

Draped over the lounging chair was her shawl, which smelled of English lavender. He dropped himself into the chair and noticed a pair of dinner plates laid on the dining table. Even though he was fairly hungry, he decided to wait for her. He felt like a solitary stream in a ravine, so far from the ocean, yet connected to it. In that rare moment of being totally alone but completely aware of another soul's presence all around, he gazed at the portrait of Christ again. How serene He looked even with that terrible suffering.

When Victoria returned, she was surprised to find Arun almost dozing in her lounging chair. 'Oh, my, you haven't eaten as yet?' she asked, as she took off her coat.

'I wanted to wait for you.'

'How was your day at the leper colony?'

'An interesting day, indeed. I met a young man from Kerala, a talented artist. He gave me this picture, which he painted with his mouth.' He unfolded the picture of the bougainvillea bush climbing over the stone wall, and to Arun's surprise, in the stone alcove he could see what looked like an unlit cigarette. He smiled to himself.

'Oh, that is a beautiful painting,' said Victoria.

Over dinner he told her the story of Raman and Methi. She listened to him intently, gazing into his eyes. 'While I was waiting for you, I was thinking of my experience at the leper colony. It was a spiritual experience for me.'

'What made you feel like that?'

'It was free from the stares of the world...the place was so peaceful.'

'Consider yourself blessed. Not many people know a leper colony exists in this valley.' And pulling out a pouch, she asked, 'Would you like to play a game of Scrabble?'

Arun had not played Scrabble since his schooldays, but after the first game, which he lost, he regained his confidence and soon he was able to arrange the letters to form words like umbrage, which surprised Victoria. She let him win the game although by a narrow margin, and this time it was Arun who asked her if she wanted to play another round even though it was getting late.

It began to rain softly at first, moistening the green foliage after many dry days. The earth emanated a wholesome odour, carried on by a light breeze that swayed the curtains. Then there was lightning that lit up the distant mountains, followed by somersaulting thunder. She grabbed his arm and then the power went off. For a moment, in pitch darkness, he was aware of only the pressure of her hand on his arm. The rain came down on the metallic roof like a steam train hissing in the wind. They could no longer hear each other.

'I have some candles in the kitchen,' she shouted. He held her hand and led her towards the kitchen. With each silvery flash of lightning, the darkness increased and then the lights came on. They found themselves holding hands.

'Do you have storms like this in England?'

'Storms are the same everywhere, even if the skies are different.' She let go of his hand. This time the lightning sizzled closer to the bungalow, and then the thunder seemed to echo across the valley. The lights went off again, and once again she held his hand. The two of them walked back to the living room with the candles. The rain was now constant and almost soporific. 'I don't want you to get wet walking to your apartment. I have an umbrella in the verandah.'

'Will you be all right on your own? It is a pity we could not finish our game of Scrabble,' said Arun.

'Maybe we can finish it tomorrow, if you have time.'

She opened the front door. A moist gust of wind blew out the candle. She held him close to her, and he felt the press of her warm body.

'Good night,' he said, as he gave her a kiss on her cheek. Momentarily her face turned towards him and her lips brushed against his.

'Good night,' she whispered. There was the smell of lavender on his cheek. He opened the umbrella and ran towards the apartment, leaping in the rain.

10

The ferocity of the storm did not hamper her movements in the darkness of the bungalow, for Victoria had dusted every nook and corner for the past fifteen years. The darkness was almost comforting. She knew the rafters let in the wind in the living room with a whistle and the gutter near her bedroom would be gurgling, the flying twigs would rattle the tin roof all night.

She wished Arun had stayed a little longer. She made her way to the bedroom and lit a candle. She blew it out as soon as she lit it and looked out from her bedroom window to see if Arun had lit a candle in his apartment. She lay in the darkness, listening to the familiar sounds. The sound of Arun's voice and laughter still resonated in her ears. In another nine months she would be listening to different voices in England. The Bishop had promised to send her to a small hamlet in Epsom Downs, not far from her brother Bert and his wife Gwenan.

She could not sleep, and a sudden void filled her. Normally, she would have listened to the BBC radio service after her prayers, which lullabied her to sleep. Often the radio would be on when she woke up in the mornings. Then it struck her that without electricity, the milk in the refrigerator would go bad. She decided to drink cold milk with Cadbury's drinking chocolate; she thought it might help her fall asleep. She missed the noisy motor of the ancient refrigerator.

As she lay in bed, she prayed to the Lord to give her direction and guidance to assuage the storm within her heart, a storm so distant in her memory, whose rumblings she had last heard in Australia. She remembered the stopover for one night she made in Singapore after she had said goodbye to Aaron in Perth. She lay in the hotel room awake, looking at the neon lights all night, unable to let go of what had been. Something she attempted to consider as past was too fresh to bury in her heart. Instead of the neon lights, she now saw a flicker of candlelight in Arun's room. How could she prevent herself from falling into this vortex again as she stood on its edge, staring at the stirrings that were throwing her off balance?

It was two o'clock in the morning, and she longed for the dawn to break. At this time of the night she could catch the BBC frequency on her little Japanese-made, yellow plastic transistor radio. The news of the mechanical failure of Big Ben and the creation of the Commission for Racial Equality in Britain did not divert her mind.

How could she think of such a thing? Arun was much younger than her. The Lord knew every thought of hers, and she knew she would not do anything without the blessing of Christ. She lit the candles again and began to read Corinthians, that beacon of morality from the Apostle Paul which comforted her. She felt a bond between herself and Arun, but she could not define it. It was nameless, without boundaries. As if in the Universe, just by chance, for a brief moment in time, two comets had come close enough to shower each other with their brightness. Unseen except by the Creator.

She took out a sheet of paper from her desk and began to write. When John came into the house, he was surprised to see the Miss Sahib at her desk. He washed the empty cup and lit the gas cooker to make the morning tea. He first warmed the china teacup just above room temperature, then put in two cubes of sugar and some warm water to make a mixture. This would draw the true flavour out of the Darjeeling teabag. Finally, a teaspoon of lukewarm milk into the cup and a gentle stir; the tea was ready.

He walked to the living room carrying a tray. 'Is everything fine, Miss Sahib?' he asked, noticing her bloodshot eyes.

'I could not sleep last night because of the terrible storm,' she responded as she folded the letter to Arun and slipped it into the Bible. 'Did you see the lightning?'

'Yes, Miss Sahib, I heard from the milkman. A few people died in the slum by the river.'

'Oh my,' she said as she gazed at the lawn strewn with litchi leaves and twigs like a forlorn battleground. If the BBC radio was her conduit to the news of the West, it was John who filled her with the local news.

'Mrs Indira Gandhi is in town,' he said nonchalantly.

'How do you know? I haven't heard anything in the news. Mind you there is not much news these days.'

'My cousin Abraham, who works as a cook at the Circuit House, told me. She likes to eat the fish called Solomon for breakfast.'

'Hmm. You mean salmon? That reminds me, John, I won't be having breakfast today. Would you please give this letter to Doctor Arun?'

❖

When Arun came for breakfast, he was surprised to see only one plate on the dining table. The bungalow was eerily quiet, except for the tick-tock of the Swiss wall clock. Beside the plate was an envelope with his name on it. He was startled by the sudden appearance of John from the kitchen who announced: 'Miss Sahib went out early today and left this envelope for you.'

Arun quickly opened the envelope and read the letter:

My love and life have to be and are naturally tempered by, modified by, affected by my spiritual life—my belief in Jesus, my life with Jesus. I cannot separate any part of what I am, or what I do, or what I hope for, from Jesus, who has given me a life of commitment, of fulfilment, of satisfaction, of joys and peace of being complete as a person. I wouldn't be here, I would not have the pleasures I've known here, I wouldn't have met the people whom I've come to love and appreciate, if it were not for Him. If I were to succumb to my natural instincts of purely personal satisfaction, I'd gain very little because I know that selfish desires bring about no permanent satisfaction.

Living with Jesus means consulting Him at every step of the way, asking, 'Is this love pure and worthy of you?' I've been reading Corinthians I during the last two weeks of my daily devotions—no coincidence—God chose to speak with me directly I'm sure, because these readings are set in my book.

I know the relationship I seek and would like to have with someone can only be found in the sanctity of marriage—within the sanctity of His blessings. This for me is now impossible; at present I have to wait and see what is in store for me.

Hence, I cannot reveal the full extent of my love, but can endeavour to prove my love in other ways. Caring, being concerned, thoughtfully helping, sharing whatever it may be. When there is sincere deep love, there is a desire to make one's beloved happier and his life a richer and more beautiful one. Under strain and stress, one fails to communicate and share love in this way, but when there is mutual love, these feelings can be forgiven and shared if openly admitted and new beginnings can be enjoyed together.

It is not easy to understand how another thinks or acts—but I do ask that you try and understand and appreciate my thoughts so that there will be no sad misunderstandings.

He read the letter again to understand its essence and this time tears rolled down his face.

'Would you like me to warm the porridge again, Doctor Sahib?' asked John as he set down a round of toasted bread.

'No thank you, John.'

'Is anything the matter, Sahib? Why are you crying?'

Arun picked up the napkin and wiped his face. 'John, at times people cry when they lose someone's friendship or trust. I am crying because I have found something, something special. You are such a good cook, not only will I miss you but Miss Sahib will also miss you a lot when she goes back to England.'

'Sahib, I too feel like crying sometimes. What shall I tell you,' he said as he sat on his haunches on the floor. 'I am hiding a secret that is weighing heavily on my heart, but you are a doctor and you will understand. I should have listened to my wife who went to heaven seven years ago. She always told me not to smoke. Now, I have maybe a year to live, the doctor told me a month ago. My lung cancer is eating my liver.'

'But, John, why are you hiding this from Miss Sahib?'

'I do not have the heart to tell her. After all these years, I want her to leave India with happy memories.'

'Have you thought about your teenage daughter?'

'Oh, yes. She wants to be a nurse. By the grace of God one day she will find a good Christian boy from the church to take care of her.' He picked up the plates. 'I hope you will not say anything to Miss Sahib.'

'If you say so John, but I think Miss Sahib has the right to know about your health,' said Arun.

John looked wistfully at the lawn. Walking outside, he began to pick up the broken branches, and then he lit a cigarette, blowing blue smoke into the stillness of the morning.

II

'To the southeast of Dehradun, in the Shivalik hills, roams an ancient tribe of nomadic herdsmen called the Gujjars,' said Dr Kumar. 'It is believed that they were part of the dowry for a Balistani princess of Nahan, and they eventually settled in those hills. Although they are Muslims who originally came from Jammu, they are vegetarians. Some believe they are descendants of the Huns, who invaded India and may have originated from Georgia.'

Dr Kumar, with his Elvis Presley-like hair, was making rounds in the hospital. He lifted a sick Gujjar child from the crib, who was listless and limp like a fish. The child had a rash, most likely Rubeola virus. Dr Kumar wore a white safari suit and spoke with youthful exuberance.

'Which one of you can tell me what the infant mortality rate might be for a Gujjar child?' asked Dr Kumar as he observed Sodi, who was admiring a student nurse with his angular glances. 'What are your thoughts, Sodi?'

'I wasn't thinking anything, Sir,' said Sodi, blushing like a rhododendron in bloom. The interns and the student nurses burst out laughing.

'Well, I want you to think for a change. What might be the IMR for this Gujjar child?'

'I would think 10 to 15 per cent, Sir,' said Sodi with a smile.

'Dr Sodi, there is a difference between a percentage and

rate. The infant mortality rate is defined as the number of infant deaths per thousand live births. I believe it is probably over two hundred for this tribe. Every year I take two interns for two weeks to the Shivalik hills for their rural posting. We track down the Gujjar families in the forest and vaccinate the infants and children. This year, I believe, I will have the pleasure of taking you and Dr Arun.'

'Sir, I have a question. Where do the female interns go for the rural posting?'

'They go to the local villages and talk about family planning and condoms and so forth.'

Sodi looked at Sujata and smiled. Scratching his forehead he said: 'Sir, I would have thought they might be better at vaccinations.'

Dr Kumar shook his head and asked Sujata the cause of high infant mortality rate.

'Sepsis and infectious diseases,' she said confidently.

'Excellent. And of course poor obstetrical care, malnutrition and so forth. If I were a microbe, India would be my heaven.' Dr Kumar turned to Arun. 'You seem to be a little lost. Did you ever find Dr Gupta's wedding rings?'

'No, Sir. I have a lot of things on my mind.'

'It seems so. Perhaps two weeks in the Shivalik hills will make you think differently.'

It would be a miracle if someone found those diamond rings on the hospital premises and returned them, Arun mused. This discourse on diseases of childhood by Dr Kumar did not hold his attention. He felt the crisp paper of Victoria's letter in his pocket. He wanted to read it again. He pictured John smoking his life away near the bungalow.

Dr Kumar continued to speak fervently about the fauna of the Shivaliks, and the Gujjars. His nose seemed to have sprouted too fast on his face, making it beak-like but still proportional to his strong jaw line.

Sujata sensed Arun's boredom and winked at him. Moving closer, she whispered: 'Tea at Dallu's?' Arun smiled.

'It is a pity Dr Kumar's wife cannot have any children,' Sujata said later, as she sipped her tea from a tall glass. 'She is beautiful, I hear.'

'How do you know all this?' inquired Arun.

'Well, they have been married for ten years for God's sake. He loves children, though.'

'Perhaps, that's why God made him a paediatrician.'

The two of them drank tea and gossiped in Dallu's tea shack, passing away the languorous afternoon.

'Do you remember the book by Ruskin Bond you brought for Vinod? Incidentally, I read a story to him that is set in the Shivalik hills. It's called "The Tiger in the Tunnel".'

'Don't tell me there are man-eating tigers in those hills.'

'Not now, you silly. But there are leopards, wild elephants and deer and, of course, the mysterious Gujjars. A few years ago when I was still at school, the wild elephants apparently rampaged and levelled a newly constructed antibiotics factory near the edge of the forest.'

'Are you trying to scare me from doing my rural posting or something?'

'Just informing, just informing,' she said, smiling.

That evening, when Arun returned to the bungalow, the lawn was immaculately clean and mowed. The green grass shone like a velvet croquet ground in the autumn sunlight. Only the players were missing. He walked to the main door, and found Victoria reading the Bible and listening to classical music.

She smiled and said, 'You are early for dinner.'

'Yes. I wanted to tell you I will be leaving for the Shivalik hills for two weeks to do my rural posting.'

Her face dropped suddenly, and then she said, 'Did you

read my letter? I hope I have not offended you in any way. I am sorry I could not join you for breakfast this morning.'

'No, no, not at all. This has nothing to do with you, really. I have been assigned with Dr Kumar and a fellow intern to vaccinate the Gujjar children.' He wanted to put his arms around her for some reason but stopped himself.

'But two weeks is a long time. I cannot believe you will be away for so long. John is making a sumptuous meal for us tonight. He managed to get some quails from somewhere. He plans to serve them with real cranberry sauce.'

'He is not just a cook. He is indeed a culinary artist.'

'So, Doctor Sahib, you better eat well and no leftovers. You know how hurt he feels on seeing leftovers.' Indeed, he thought, remembering the numerous times he had left piles of food on his plate. Arun knew that John made each meal as if it might be the last meal he would cook. Ironically, Victoria was unaware of his diagnosis, and he was bound by the promise he made to John.

'You don't seem very happy today for some reason,' she said, extending her hand and touching his wrist. 'I hope you understand my feelings. It's not that I...' she stopped when John brought in two bowls of piping hot tomato soup with fresh cream.

Arun said, 'After two weeks I am not sure if I will be allowed to continue at the hospital, unless I pay three thousand rupees for Dr Gupta's wedding rings. Was there any mail for me?'

'Not that I know of. Were you expecting something?'

'I wrote to my mother in England to send me money.'

Victoria put down her spoon and cupped her chin with her hand. 'Why did you ask your mother? She is struggling in a foreign country as it is.'

Arun became aware of slurping his soup as the conversation ended. The meal was delicious. He made sure that he ate every bit of the quail, including the bones, which were quite soft. John was applauded for his fine work, and as he cleared the china plates he felt he had lived another fulfilling day.

When Arun got up to leave, Victoria said, 'Wait!' She returned with an envelope in her hand. 'Please give this cheque to Dr Gupta's husband. This money will be of no use to me in England.'

Arun opened the envelope and held the cheque gingerly in his hands, weighed by the burden of gratitude, but it was the weight of love that made his eyes well up.

'Thank you,' he said softly embracing her. She looked at his watery eyes.

'Don't be silly,' she said shaking her head.

❖

The road to the Shivalik hills cuts straight through the Doon Valley, with fields of barley and sugarcane on either side. The humble greenish-blue peaks, like identical triangles, rise gently from the earth pointing to the sky. Dr Kumar's ancient white Ambassador car smelled of old leather and gasoline.

Sodi stretched himself on the back seat using his turban as a pillow. Soon after crossing the city, the chaotic traffic waned, but Dr Kumar used his foot on the brakes every now and then, even on the clear road, perhaps to assure himself the brakes were in order. Arun felt quite nauseated in the front passenger seat.

'My boys, you are going to have the time of your life. I have bottles of Golden Eagle beer in the icebox, along with the vaccine,' said Dr Kumar. 'I have the Old Monk Triple X rum for the forest ranger. It has never failed to get me the best hospitality. Do you know the Indian soldiers swear by it? The Triple X tastes better the higher you are on a mountain. Oh, look!'

Dr Kumar slammed on the brakes, his face in child-like awe. 'That is the great Indian hornbill feeding its mate,' he whispered. 'The male imprisons its mate in the nest, which is sealed by plaster made of its faeces, until the chicks grow. See how he is feeding the female through that hole.'

He switched off the car. The forest of sal trees and pines echoed with the sound of the cicadas. The greenery cast shimmering shadows on the dirt road.

'Have you ever had a frightening experience in this forest?' asked Arun.

'I have never been frightened by the big cats or elephants, but a couple of years ago a King Cobra scared me like hell when I came across him, face to face in the middle of the dirt road near a dry riverbed.'

'I hate snakes,' said Sodi, sitting upright. 'So what did you do?'

'Well, I did not make any sudden moves. I stared straight into his eyes and glided my right leg up to my thigh and stood on one leg like Lord Shiva. I reckoned if he came too close I would stomp him under my right foot. I stood my ground, he simply slithered away to the bushes.'

The sun was beginning to go down. A colony of monkeys darted in between the trees. The cry of a barking deer came across the valley. 'But where are the Gujjars?' asked Arun.

'They are deep in the valley, not far from the Forest Rest house. They roam these pastures with their cattle and supply milk to the city. Do you know they treat their cattle with the same affection as they do their children?'

It was almost dark by the time they reached the rest house near a tributary of the Yamuna River. The small bungalow with slanted roof was dwarfed by giant trees. The forest ranger came out holding an oil lantern in his hand and a blanket across his shoulders. His features were distinctly Nepali. His army cap bore the brass emblem of two kukris crossed together. Dr Kumar showed him the permit for the rest house. He opened the boot of the car and carefully took out the large bottle of Old Monk. 'This is for you,' he said. The ranger's lined face exploded into a smile.

The rest house, like so many long-forgotten remains of remote British outposts, surprised one with remnants like the veneered walnut furniture. At the first light, the ranger woke them up to see the elephants feeding near the river. The fog had not yet lifted from the ground across the river and they seemed to be floating in the air.

'Now, are you ready for some serious work my boys?' said Dr Kumar as he took a photograph with his Canon camera, 'We will wade through the river—it's not very deep—to those huts on the other side.'

The elephants walked as if in slow motion to the grove of trees and waited with heads bowed as if in communion before the feast. Arun's mind was awash not with the elephants, but with the image of John walking in slow motion and Victoria saying Grace before breakfast. She was immured in her love of Christ—or did she let herself wander and think about him at this very moment? He looked up at the solitary eagle soaring on wind currents above the mountains, and he longed to be transported in the folds of Garuda's wings back to Victoria's bungalow.

The riverbed was dry in parts, with tentacles of tributaries that made little islands in the heart of the river. On one of the islands stood a perfectly round mud hut, with a goat tied in front of it. 'That hut you see over there,' said the ranger, 'is called a dera by the Gujjars. They build them on small islands to keep away the wild animals. Please respect their privacy when we enter the hut.'

Puffs of smoke floated from the top of the slanted roof. At first it seemed deserted. Dr Kumar placed his finger across his lips to indicate that they should keep their voices down. A tall fair woman with emerald eyes emerged from the hut carrying two infants, one on each hip. As soon as she saw the forest ranger, she was at ease.

'Doctors from town have come to see your children,' said the ranger.

She smiled and pulled a veil over her face and ushered them to come inside the hut. A fire crackled in a makeshift pit of rounded stones in the middle of the floor. Six or seven bare-bottomed children chewed on wild berries. Rusted metal trunks stood in one corner with a pile of blankets on top. 'My twins have pus coming out of both ears for many days. They cry all night,' she said, looking at the ranger.

Dr Kumar gently inspected the ears of the twins, who were surprisingly docile and wide-eyed. 'Deafness for sure if left untreated,' he whispered.

'What do we do, Sir? We do not have any liquid antibiotics,' said Sodi.

'Can I do anything to help, Dr Sahib?' asked the ranger.

Dr Kumar put his arm on the ranger's shoulder. 'You are the only one who can help. If we give you fifty rupees, would you go to Dehradun to purchase the antibiotics and promise us you will deliver them to these children? Otherwise they will become not only deaf but also mute.'

The ranger opened his shirt and showed a large scar across his chest. 'I am a military man who fought for my country. You know I have lost two young sons fighting the war in Kashmir. Money means nothing to me, Sir. Trust means everything.'

'Of course, of course!' said Dr Kumar.

'I have fifty rupees,' said Arun.

'Can you write a prescription for some Amoxycillin elixir? This is one prescription that you will remember all your life, my boy.'

12

It was late in the afternoon when Dr Gupta got home. The smell of the anaesthetic gases had given her a pulsating headache. The afternoon sun shone with a silvery glare. She drew the curtains of the kitchen window. Her mother-in-law's lunch plate lay untouched on the counter. She heard the familiar unbalanced heavy footsteps of her mother-in-law behind her. She turned around. Her mother-in-law's lips were pouting, strung up by the billowing creases of her face.

'Why haven't you eaten your lunch?'

There was no answer. The old lady opened the cabinet, picked up a glass and turned on the tap and let the water run until it became cooler.

'I am talking to you, why haven't you eaten your lunch?'

'Do you care if I eat or not? You know I don't like Ramu kneading the dough for me. I would do it myself if it did not make me so breathless. Rakesh and I were surviving before you came into this house. I can take care of myself.'

Her words got on Nasreen's nerves.

'Where is Ramu?' Nasreen asked her mother-in-law.

'I fired him today. You know how these servants are these days. Good for nothing. He thought he could make some money with the groceries I ordered. I knew his chaal and caught him red-handed. Can you make me some tea before you change your clothes?'

The old lady shifted her eyes to gauge her daughter-in-law's reaction, her reptilian eyes deep in her sockets from years of observation and inference. Her torso tilted to one side as if barely hinged to her pelvis. She limped to the backyard to sit in the October sun. 'Don't forget to put some ginger in the tea,' she said as she bolted the back door.

Nasreen thought, why can't she make the tea herself? There was a peculiar smell in the kitchen. Her nose felt blocked, and her head seemed too heavy for her slender neck. Ginger, ginger, where was the damn ginger? Now that Ramu was gone, she would have to bow to her mother-in-law's every whim and command. His rusted metal suitcase in the pantry, where he slept, was gone. He had forgotten to take his towel which hung on the inside handle of the pantry door. He must have left in a hurry, forsaking his beloved brass statue of Ganesh covered in the incense ash of his spent prayers and chants.

The kitchen felt eerily quiet. Every morning after using the bathroom in the garden shed, Ramu would take a cold shower with the garden hose and come into the kitchen for his prayers and chanting, much to the delight of the mother-in-law. She made him shave his head every morning so as to prevent any hair falling into the food he cooked. Now there would be no Ramu for the old lady to nag, no more jabs of sarcasm to the twenty-year-old from Nepal about his caste, his demeanour or his trustworthiness. Did he head back to Nepal or was he sitting like a forlorn traveller at some railway platform? Now there would be more of bring me this, bring me that, or why can't you get pregnant.

Standing before the glass window, she saw little boys with gleaming wet skins diving into the canal that flowed across the road, giggling, cajoling each other to see who could stay underwater the longest. She heard the sonorous voice of the vegetable-seller hawking his produce. How could she get pregnant? For one thing, her husband was always away from home defending illegal mining tycoons in the courts of Delhi. She felt as barren and scarred as the quarried hills of the valley. The hospital Superintendent had told her it was the anaesthetic gases of the operating room messing up her cycles. She knew her mother-in-law would never believe that, so she never told her.

Nasreen put the pan over the gas stove. Then she lit the match.

A sheet of fire engulfed her. She ran towards the door and felt something melt on her back. Through the orange cloud of fire, she gave a thunderous cry, begging someone to open the door. The synthetic sari melted around her legs, searing her skin. Black smoke filled her lungs. Floundering in the swirling sea of fire and smoke, she crawled towards the door. Desperately, she tried to peel off the molten blobs of nylon from her body, or what was left of her clothing. Her long hair, groomed with coconut oil, caught fire and shrivelled into spaghetti-like rings on top of her head.

She kicked the door open, unleashing revolving tunnels of smoke that embraced her mother-in-law. Nearly naked, she ran towards the canal across the road and jumped into the water.

At first the young boys bathing in the canal were amused to see an Egyptian mummy-like woman, naked and blackened without any hair or eyebrows, stumble into the canal like a drunk with smoke coming out of her nostrils. But soon they realized something was amiss when they saw fire around the window from the house across the road. A crowd gathered around the house. Someone commandeered the pushcart of the vegetable seller and placed a couple of buckets to fetch water from the canal. Soon police jeeps and an ancient fire truck pulled up. The little boys pointed to the naked woman floating in the canal.

Inspector Yadav sniffed the air and rested his foot on the ledge of the canal, watching his subordinates pull out the body. He was back to the mundane tasks of apprehending petty criminals and investigating kitchen fires. The last few weeks had been full of excitement. He loved to barge into the walled bungalows of Rajpur Road where the political enemies of Mrs Indira Gandhi had holed up. He loved to say: 'Sir, you are under arrest under Article 352 of the Constitution of India.' The men always complied and sat in his jeep with glum faces. It was the women of the house he detested, because he couldn't say anything without them making a scene. One politician's wife had the gall to set her dogs loose upon him.

'Shamsher Singh, cover her up for God's sake!' he ordered.

'Sir, do you suspect foul play?'

'In a kitchen fire, there is always some khel, Shamsher Singh. Do you know, twenty-five thousand women die each year in kitchen fires? Most of them are newlyweds under the age of twenty-five. There is always some foul khel. Who else was in the house?'

'Only the mother-in-law. But the old lady is also overcome with the smoke and barely breathing.'

'Where is her husband?'

'I believe he left for Delhi two days ago.'

'Any servants?'

'I am not sure, Sir. All I know is, it is a curse to be born as a girl in India. In the month of March I investigated the death of a newborn female. This woman, Sir, gave birth to twins, a boy and a girl, and the next morning she claimed the baby girl died naturally. But, Sir, you know what happened. The doctor called it cot death.'

❖

At the hospital, there was collective grief. The nurses hugged each other, wailing; the young interns stood in corners, weeping as Dr Gupta's body was taken to the Emergency Room.

Arun put his arms around the pillar, where once Dr Gupta had stood with him, demanding her wedding rings. Her mother-in-law, whom she feared so much, had also died in the ambulance as it meandered through the traffic. Tears bubbled in his eyes and he lost focus of all that was around him. All he could hear in his mind was 'where are my wedding rings Dr Arun? My mother-in-law will kill me'. His legs began to shake. He slid down the pillar. He stared at the pillar with its peeled plaster and saw shapes—a mother carrying a child, a pointed church spire with a cross, or was it a face he could not recognize? It was the piercing side glance from Trishna as she turned her face away and pointed her nose to the sky that jumpstarted his heart into a frenzy. He dug his fingernails into the plaster and began to cry.

Trishna stepped towards him, and asked: 'Why did this happen? This horrific death?'

Arun looked towards the peepul tree where the birds and chirpy sparrows were settling in the branches, bathed in purple twilight. 'Why does anything happen? I wish I knew the answer,' he said, as his eyes searched for the silhouettes of the birds in the tree.

'What are you looking at?' she asked him.

'We are either living life, or we are just witnesses to it, that's all,' he said.

'What do you mean?'

'I wish I had never come to Dehradun.'

'I don't understand. This has nothing to do with you. It was an accident.'

'Accident or murder?'

'Shhh,' said Trishna, putting her finger on his lips, 'don't say this, you will get into trouble for starting a rumour. I was supposed to assist her in the operating room tomorrow. Can I come and see you at your place this evening? I have something very important to tell you.'

'Why don't you tell me now? I mean, of course, you can come and see me,' he said, his face warming with a blush. She had been to his apartment thrice, but the memory of the last visit was still fresh, and for days afterward he could not look at her straight.

'No, can you meet me at Topekeshwar Temple this evening? Be sure to be there at five.'

❖

Topekeshwar Temple was not really a temple but a cave in a rock face on the outskirts of the city. Trishna had taken him there when they had first met and they had held hands inside the dark cave, which had a stalagmite for a Shivalingam. It was lit by a single oil wick. An ageless, sage-like old man with a flowing white beard, a self-appointed guardian of the temple, usually stood outside, tending the hanging ferns on the rock, facing the waters of the mountain stream whilst young lovers or devotees venerated the crystalline lingam. She had made a secret wish here on their first visit, and she would not tell him what it was because it would not be fulfilled if she revealed it.

The unconventional temple had a magical spell. The fast-flowing stream over the boulders near the cave roared with the ferocity of life, and inside the cave was the stillness of the bowels of the earth. Where there was meant to be no light, an orange light bounced off the smooth rocks full of iron ore. The intoxicating smell of incense escaped through the sweat pores, and it was easy to lose not only oneself but also time.

As they stood next to each other in front of the Shivalingam, Arun prayed for the soul of Dr Gupta. Trishna closed her eyes, her face serene and glowing, and then she opened her eyes and turned towards him. He wondered what she was about to tell him. As he lowered his eyes, a thought flashed at the back of his mind. Was she about to say she was married before or she was getting engaged to someone? He raised his eyes to look at her; her eyelashes seemed too heavy for her, weighted down with moisture. 'You wanted to tell me something important, Trishna, didn't you?'

She did not answer him. She took a deep breath and held his arm. 'I am so afraid, afraid of everything.'

'Afraid of what?'

'Of you, and me.'

'But you still haven't told me what you wanted to.'

'Perhaps; you will understand one day. I cannot bear to be at work now. I am going back home for a couple of weeks.' There was a reverberating cough at the mouth of the cave: the sage reminding them their prayer was perhaps too long. They emerged from the cave under the canopy of trees with green sunlight. The sage raised his hands to bless them. But Arun's heart was as restless as the silvery stream babbling towards the ravine.

13

Mr Gupta who was used to speaking in court with fervour now sat at the police station, facing Inspector Yadav in a rickety chair, as a silent listener. In the courts, it was he who asked barbed questions to policemen and the accused in a self-assured voice, pacing up and down and opening his palms as if to reveal the truth that he had been holding delicately; but now it was he who answered questions asked by the inspector and other men in uniform in monotonous monosyllables.

He could not believe what tide had brought him to this shore, from where he could see through the looking-glass the point from where he was carried away, and he muttered to himself, remembering Maupassant again. Was it a dream?

'And these are your house keys?' said Inspector Yadav as he managed to open his drawer after multiple attempts. 'I am sorry to inform you of this terrible tragedy, Sir, but we have the culprit in our custody. We were lucky to apprehend him before he was able to board the train to Delhi.'

'Who might that be?' asked Mr Gupta, a little startled by this revelation. He paced back and forth in the small office of the inspector who looked at him with some annoyance.

'None other than your servant Ramu,' said the inspector.

'That cannot be true. I just cannot believe he had anything to do with this accident.'

'Sir, accident it was, but a deliberate accident, if you know what I mean. I deal with criminals every day.'

'I deal with them myself, Inspector. What proof do you have?'

'Proof?'

The inspector opened the drawer again and pulled out typed sheets from his folder, flicking them on to the table like a hand of cards. Had Mr Gupta not been a lawyer, his patience might have been thin. 'Sir, he signed a confession. We did have the usual difficulty, but suspension by the ankles into the drum with salt water usually works. Your mother made a statement in the ambulance, she had fired Ramu that morning and he must have left the gas cylinder on with the intent to kill her. He not only killed your mother but your wife as well. Don't you think he deserves to go to hell?'

Little drops of sweat broke out on Mr Gupta's forehead, and he found it hard to control his shaking knee. He got up and pushed the papers towards the inspector.

'May I have the keys to my house?'

'Certainly,' said the inspector.

When Mr Gupta left the police station, the sky darkened with billowing grey clouds. The wind rustled the tree leaves and swayed the overhead electric lines in a chaotic rhythm. The impending thunder he felt was not from the sky but within him and it made him shudder. He drove to the post office to collect his mail. One envelope caught his eye. It was from the office of the Principal of the Girls' Christian School.

The sudden downpour caught everyone unawares and he pulled his car into a side alley. A homeless beggar woman with a baby on her hip ran for cover and still managed to knock at his car with futile hope. He opened the letter.

There was a cheque for three thousand rupees, signed Victoria Lambert, Principal, Christian Girls' School, and a short note from Dr Arun which read:

Dear Mr Gupta,

I am sorry I cannot replace Dr Gupta's wedding rings. She did hand them to me but I do not remember anything after the unfortunate incident at the hospital. I am truly sorry for the loss which means so much to you both.

Mr Gupta carefully folded the note and the cheque. He wondered why a European lady had written a cheque on behalf of Dr Arun. The cheque and the rings seemed immaterial to him now that Nasreen and his mother were gone, and he felt as arid and empty as an ancient riverbed. He listened to the pelting rain on his car and the whine of his ferocious windscreen wipers. He felt as homeless as the beggar woman with the baby and suddenly he wept the kind of tears that flow without crying.

He ran to the woman who had taken refuge under the tree across the road, and emptied his wallet into her hands. Then he drove to see Ravi, his cousin, his only relative in town who had moved from Delhi to start an up-and-coming practice as an architect. It was Ravi who had designed the one-storey bungalow for his mother. He was afraid to drive home and go into the house on his own, but he also was afraid to take Ravi with him, in case Nasreen had left some epitaphic note or a diary of her true feelings for him. He wondered if she had truly loved him.

As soon as the storm abated, he drove back to the police station. Inspector Yadav was taking off his belt to change into civilian clothes.

'Inspector Yadav, I want to talk to Ramu,' said Mr Gupta.

'Sir, he is in the hawalad. It is not possible today.'

'Very well, I will see him tomorrow. Do you want me to get a court order?'

'That won't be necessary, Sir.' The inspector saw the urgency in his eyes and the edginess in his step. He decided to drive him personally to the cell housing Ramu.

As he was not a criminal lawyer, Mr Gupta never had the need to visit a prison in his life. Like all old buildings, court houses and hospitals, the prison too had a distinct odour, which was so alien to his nostrils, a sort of odour of failed human flotsam that overpowered him. He quickened his steps through the dark, damp corridors. The inspector ran his baton across the bars of the prison cells as he walked along, the sound echoing in the corridor, much to the annoyance of Mr Gupta. Ramu lay on his side in the dark cell.

'Get up!' barked Inspector Yadav, prodding him with his baton.

'I would like to speak to him alone, Inspector, if you don't mind.'

'Very well. You only have a few minutes.'

Ramu uncoiled himself but he staggered as he tried to stand up on his weakened ankles, and held on to the bars.

'Why did you leave the gas cylinder on?' asked Mr Gupta softly.

Ramu did not answer for a while then, tears flowing down his bruised and misshapen cheeks, he said, 'I swear on Bhagwan Krishan, I have not done anything. I always shut the gas cylinder. Please believe me.'

Mr Gupta took out the sheaf of papers from his pocket. 'You signed these papers.'

'They beat me,' he said lifting his shirt to show the purple bruises of the baton marks on his back. 'I don't know how this happened, Sahib. I am innocent, Sahib, please believe me.'

After hearing what Ramu had said, and what he had wanted to hear, Mr Gupta stood there looking into Ramu's eyes and listening to the noise of roosting pigeons in the rafters, until the inspector told him it was time to leave.

❖

Mr Gupta took a circuitous route to the town and drove around the Clock Tower several times, then turned onto the road towards the cantonment at the opposite end of the town. He had not faced many battles before, except for coming to terms with his father's death when he was a teenager. He had never fallen or been betrayed by love or experienced any pangs of longing.

Nasreen had walked into his life as if by some divine coincidence. His life had been a serene river for most of its course which now seemingly ended into a waterfall. Suddenly he felt so alone. There was a dust cloud over the parade ground where the soldiers had been marching. There was hardly any civilian traffic; the wide tree-lined road was deserted. He stopped the car and walked towards its trunk. From under a pile of legal papers, he picked up a bag and got back into the car. He opened the bag carefully and unscrewed a bottle of Scotch. He sipped it slowly for a long time and then set his half-empty bottle on the dashboard.

He took a wrong turn to the East Canal road as if he had already forgotten his way to the house. The blackened façade of the house seemed like a relic of the past, tomb-like and desolate. He hesitated to go in. The house was peculiar as the kitchen faced the canal and the road. The living room and the dining room were in the middle and the bedrooms were at the back, facing the garden. He staggered into the living room which was covered in soot. Surprisingly, the bedrooms were untouched by the fire. When he opened his wife's wardrobe, it still held her familiar odour.

The whiskey was getting to his head and the air felt heavy in his nostrils as he walked into his mother's bedroom. There was a stillness to the air since the fire. The valuables of three generations of his family were in a secret chamber behind his mother's bed, to which he did not bother to have access while she was alive. He did not have the key to the big padlock that was specially made for her by a master locksmith in Saharanpur. But the hinges were rusty, and when he kicked the door, the hinges came off.

There was a blue velvet blanket on which lay numerous white knotted handkerchiefs. His mother had the habit of tying the jewellery in handkerchiefs, but he noticed a newer-looking yellow satin handkerchief. The cloth was slippery and the knots were tight, but when he untied them he fell to his knees. He had found Nasreen's wedding rings. He held them in his hands and slowly closed his fingers and held them tightly. All this time, his mother had chastised Nasreen for the loss and he had remained quiet, as always, in front of his mother.

The horror of fire engulfing Nasreen made him faint. Nasreen had taken many breaths in this house and he began to take deep breaths, hoping to breathe the same air she had once breathed. His palms pressed against the rings tighter until the pain became like a numbness that spread to his heart. He began to murmur to himself again and again... was it a dream, was it a dream.

14

'Don't be depressed, Arun yaar,' said Sodi, reassuringly. 'Her death is a shock for all of us. What can you do? Nothing. It was her kismet.'

'Do you remember, she told me it was a bad omen to lose the wedding rings? Her words still haunt me,' said Arun.

'Do you really believe in omens?'

'Not really.'

'Listen, I have a plan. It is Friday...how about we ride on my motorbike to see my school friend, Binny, in Chakrata? Free booze at almost 8,000 feet, man! What a view of the sparkling Himalayas!'

'How come the booze is free?'

'Well, you see, Binny was at school with me. His dad is a colonel in the Army. He really wanted him to become a doctor, but Binny, you know, was happy-go-lucky and couldn't get into pre-med. But he has not done badly, not at all. He supplies meat to the Army.'

'So he is a contractor of sorts?'

'Exactly; only because of his father's connections in the Army.'

'It seems I am the only one without any connections. I wonder if I will ever get a surgical house job in Delhi.'

'Forget it, yaar, either you have to prove you are a Dalit, or your grandfather was a freedom fighter, or you know some political bigwig; otherwise, forget it. You should go to England.'

'What will you do, Sodi?'

'Oh, probably join the Army, and knowing my luck, I will be posted to some remote place in Ladakh.'

That afternoon, when Arun went to tell Victoria he was going away for the weekend, she showed a subtle reservation. For one, she thought it was not a good idea to ride a motorbike all the way to Chakrata. Besides, she had invited Reverend Phillips to dinner to help Arun get over the tragedy by praying together.

John stood there in the shadows waiting for the verdict, for he had made Anglo-Indian egg curry which was a favourite of Reverend Phillips.

Arun was adamant. 'I really need to go out of town to clear my mind.'

When she realized he couldn't be dissuaded, she gave him her woollen scarf and watched him go until he disappeared beyond the litchi grove.

The two young men drove out of town on a Rajdoot motorbike. They passed the baroque buildings of the Forest Research Institute and the National Defence Academy. The traffic dwindled to an occasional bullock cart loaded with sugarcane, and the air felt exhilarating against their faces, except when a decrepit interstate bus passed them, spewing diesel fumes and an occasional spray of vomit. The flat of the land slowly gave way to rolling hills. There were dry riverbeds with polished stones which the road cut through.

'This is called an Irish bridge,' said Sodi.

'How come?'

'Well, the road is on the riverbed, and during the rainy season the water just flows over the road.'

'No doubt the British coined this name.'

In the distance, the wooded slopes of the foothills of the Himalayas shrouded in mist came into view. The gentle incline gave way to the twists and turns of the mountain road. The military trucks, loaded with supplies, straining in grinding low gear were easy to pass by. Halfway up the mountain, the road forked into a restricted area. At the entrance were a few roadside Tibetan restaurants with their fluttering prayer flags. The valley below, covered with haze, looked serene.

The wind was getting cooler by every turn of the road as they gained altitude. The hairpin bend brought into view the stunning permanent snowline as the sun was setting. The peaks, like timeless golden pagodas, seemed to be suspended against the pale blue sky. It was almost midnight by the time they got through the security checkpoints, manned by solitary Gurkha soldiers, along the single lane to the military area.

The momos at the roadside Tibetan restaurant hadn't done much for their appetite, and they were both hungry like schoolboys. Binny appeared at the last security checkpoint with open arms, wearing army fatigues. He sported a Charles Branson-type goatee. Instead of wearing a turban, he had a cap on his head.

'Welcome doctors, welcome my friends, welcome to Shangrila!' he said hugging Sodi, the way long-lost school friends do. As he hugged him, he lifted Sodi up and showered good old Punjabi expletives concerning his sister.

'This is Arun.'

'Hello, my friend. You are shivering. I have just the right stuff to warm you up.'

He led them down the hill to a cottage facing the mountains. His Nepali orderly, Thapa, had lit a roaring Canadian stove above which stood an aluminium kettle.

The wood-panelled walls were adorned with posters of Bob Marley and Rajesh Khanna with Mumtaz. In the corner was a small bookshelf stocked with novels by James Hadley Chase and Alistair MacLean.

'It is so nice to see you guys! It can get rather lonely here at this altitude,' he said, opening a bottle of whiskey. 'Soda or hot water?'

'Hot water for everyone, I think,' said Sodi.

A full moon hung over the snowy mountains, bathing them in a silvery glow. Arun made himself comfortable in front of the fire and tried not to think about Dr Gupta or Trishna. He gulped down the whiskey in one shot, which made Binny arch his eyebrows as he looked at Arun in pleasant disbelief.

'To our friendship,' he said, pouring himself a rather large peg.

'So how do you keep yourself busy here?' asked Arun.

'Well, I drive my truck to the neighbouring villages to procure livestock for the Army. Sometimes, I wish I had made it to the medical field as my father wanted, not for his sake, but for the poverty and the lack of medical care I see in the villages. It is disheartening,' he said, lifting the whiskey glass against the light. 'You know, I just missed the selection by 2 per cent.'

'But you are happy, aren't you?' asked Sodi.

'Well, I make good money. I love the solitude of the Himalayas, which you guys will crave one day, but everything else is scarce here at this altitude, happiness or sadness—including women.'

'Don't talk about women. Our friend Arun is depressed because the girl he loves is carrying on with an Army man, and the one who loves him he is not sure about, and on top of that, our colleague died in a freak accident.'

Binny's speech was decidedly slurred as he went to fetch another bottle of whiskey from under his bed. 'I have to tell you this Ghalib couplet,' he said:

An ideal city for you and I
Is none
Somewhere there is no land
Elsewhere there is no sky…

'That is so profound, Binny,' said Arun, his eyes brimming with tears. 'It seems we have our lives in front of us, searching for that elusive city. Perhaps I should marry Trishna after all.'

'Who is Trishna?' asked Binny.

'She is a nurse who works with me.'

'A nurse who works with you,' he said with a sarcastic laugh. 'Who wants to marry a nurse?'

Arun's face glowed in front of the fire. He took another sip of the whiskey, and another batch of tears rolled down his cheeks. He remembered the last meeting with Trishna, her turmoil over the brevity of their relationship and the fragility of their feelings. 'Binny, it is the person one marries and not the profession.'

'Don't get senti, yaar. That is the truth. You must be hungry.'

'We had some momos at the Tibetan cafe,' said Sodi.

'You mean area 22?'

'What is area 22?'

'You don't know area 22? Maybe I shouldn't be telling you about it. It is, my friends, the secret CIA facility to train Tibetan dissidents and slip them into China to do subversive stuff like rescue the monks from Tibet and blow up bridges. We should be grateful we have a country, even if it's a country with flaws,' said Binny, curling his wrists in drunken abandon and eyeing his Nepali orderly, who was busy stoking the fire—the only person who was sober in the room. Binny seemed like a man who had recovered from cabin fever, a cabin which was well stocked with liquor. He was getting increasingly garrulous.

Sodi suddenly realized he was extremely hungry and announced: 'You know what I really fancy eating right now?

'What?' asked Binny.

'Brain curry, because I do not want a hangover.'

'Thapa has made goat curry, but, heck, brain curry is no problem, no problem at all. You know I am a meat supplier.' He instructed Thapa to go down to the yard where goats were kept and slaughter a goat. It was three o'clock in the morning. Half an hour later Thapa came back with the severed head of a goat held by the ears, which he cracked open. Arun was the first one to throw up as he saw Thapa extract the jelly-like brain. Binny was already snoring in a corner. Sodi was the only one without a hangover in the morning.

15

Reverend Phillips stood at the pulpit with his hand outstretched as if he was grasping something in the air. He had paused after saying the word *love*, and then he continued about the love of Christ. The schoolgirls in the front rows listened to him intently as he spoke about the woman of ill repute in the house of Simon, who had washed the feet of Jesus and caressed his feet with her hair as Simon looked on in disdain. He spoke about the Lord's forgiveness, a quality that he said humans lacked and needed to be reminded of constantly.

It was precisely this forgiveness that Mr Gupta was seeking, sitting unobtrusively at the back of the church. The only European in the congregation, sitting a couple of rows ahead of him, he surmised, was the English missionary who had written the cheque to him on behalf of Dr Arun. She was wearing a blue polka-dot dress; her reddish-brown hair was a sharp contrast to her fair, freckled skin. Reverend Phillips told the congregation not to be judgmental, as those who claim to be self-righteous often carry the burden of sin in their minds.

Although Mr Gupta had seen many churches, he had never been inside one. He felt a certain kind of peace that he had never felt in a temple. There was no incense here, no bells or idols, or the chanting of Sanskrit shlokas. He was wearing his shoes, but he still felt the collective goodness of the people around him, and his heart was as calm as the still air currents that lift eagles to great heights on a summer's day. His heart too was soaring to Reverend Phillips's soothing voice.

He took out his wallet from his pocket and opened it partially to look at the picture of his wife. The congregation stood up to sing a hymn. A girl from the front row went on to the stage to play the piano. The light that filtered through the blue-and-orange stained-glass windows cast a spell upon him. Somehow, he felt the presence of his wife, but it was only the warm orange light that was caressing him. He did not want the service to end. Reverend Phillips became just a blur in the distance as he closed his eyes to lose himself to the crescendo of the hymn.

Victoria stood next to the wisteria bush that was climbing the yellow wall of the church. She chatted with the girls from her orphanage, and every now and then the girls burst into laughter. Mr Gupta tried to make himself inconspicuous but Reverend Phillips' sharp eyes had spotted the new member of the congregation. He walked up to him to shake his hand. 'Welcome to our church. You must be new to the area?'

'Actually, I have lived here all my life, although this is the first time I have been inside this church. Or any church for that matter.'

'It is the Lord's calling. May His blessings be upon you. May the sun always shine upon your face,' said Reverend Phillips, cupping Mr Gupta's hand between his.

'Thank you, Reverend. I would like to meet Miss Lambert.'

'Oh, sure. What is your name?'

'Rakesh Gupta.'

'And what do you do, if I may ask?'

'I am a lawyer.'

The Reverend's smile somewhat withered to an expression of concern. 'Is everything all right?'

'Yes, of course. It's just a personal matter.'

Victoria had started walking with the girls on the gravel path to the school. The Reverend called after her. He rested his hand on Mr Gupta's shoulder and quickened his pace. By the time they caught up with Victoria, the Reverend was breathless. 'This is Mr Gupta, a lawyer. He would like to speak with you.'

Victoria turned around and saw a tall, handsome man with fine features in a pinstriped suit. For a moment, she was not sure if he was Dr Gupta's husband.

'I am Rakesh Gupta, Madam.'

'You may call me Victoria,' she said.

'Well, Victoria, you wrote this cheque for me,' he said, taking out his wallet. 'It was supposed to be from Dr Arun.'

'Yes, of course. I am terribly sorry to hear about your wife...and your mother.'

'Thank you. I wish to return this cheque to you.'

'Perhaps you should return it to Dr Arun. He will be back from Chakrata this evening.'

Mr Gupta stood there looking at her smooth forehead and bright blue eyes. He extended his hand to give her the cheque. A sudden gust of wind blew the cheque out of his hand and into the shrubbery. Retrieving it from a thorn bush, he said, 'I have no reason to replace my wedding rings. You may find it hard to believe me, but I had no intention of encashing this cheque anyway.'

The wind was billowing Victoria's skirt and she struggled to hold it down. She wanted to take the cheque and walk away, but she found herself uncertain as he held her in his honest gaze.

'When I received the cheque from you, I was a little puzzled. The more I found out about you and the work you do, the more ashamed I felt of myself. Dr Arun was not at fault, not at all. Some things just happen.'

Reverend Phillips chatted with the parishioners. Every now and then he cast a cursory look towards Victoria and Mr Gupta, who seemed to be in deep conversation. The Reverend was an Indian Christian, a darkish middle-aged man with handsome features, who grew up in Saharanpur. Three years ago, the diocese had offered him a position to preach in Canada. At the time, it seemed the opportunity of a lifetime for him, his wife, and his two young kids. It was the Lord's calling. Of course, they knew Canada would be very cold, but he did not anticipate the vastness and the desolation of small-town Canada. Just south of Winnipeg, on the border with America, the Reverend preached to cattle herders and farmers of Nordic stock, who could barely understand his accent. The unending parallel roads bisecting swaths of land made him feel minute. The brutal snowstorms and blizzards of biblical proportions would have humbled even the great explorer, Ernest Shackleton. It was in this loneliness that he longed for the broken, winding roads of his homeland; the hustle and bustle of roadside vendors; of people walking around, oblivious to the squalor; the reassuring sounds of the rickshaw bells and car horns; the soothing sound of Sunday church bells; and the smell of dust and passing rain showers. By God's grace he was back in familiar surroundings and now each human being seemed special to him.

He walked towards the English missionary and Mr Gupta. 'I hope I am not intruding. Did you enjoy the service?'

'Very much so, Reverend,' said Mr Gupta.

'Then I hope to see you again this Sunday.'

'Of course, Reverend. I have a lot to learn from you.'

'I also learn from people,' said Reverend Phillips with a smile.

Mr Gupta stayed back for a while and watched the cheery flowerbeds of morning glories and petunias fluttering in the wind along the gravel path of the church. Soon the congregation began to dissipate as people walked away. Deep inside, his soul felt trampled with the sound of each footstep on the path. He stopped walking, and looked back at the empty church as he stood alone. He felt besotted by the dark thoughts reminding him about Nasreen and his mother, his charred house, the canal and the policeman. Reverend Phillips' voice reverberated in his head, 'The Father of mercies, the god of all comfort; who comforteth us in all our tribulations.' He cried out, 'Oh my Lord.' Then drove to the prison to see Ramu.

16

Arun seldom walked into the bungalow other than at meal times. But he was hungry after the long trip from Chakrata. There was no one else in the bungalow except for John at this time of the day. The afternoon shadow of the peepul tree cut the shimmering sunlight into bits on top of the roof. Arun opened the creaky front door with its wire meshing to keep the flies and mosquitoes out.

It was dark inside the bungalow. He could hear John working in the kitchen, chopping onions or vegetables. There was the smell of a cold kitchen, washed mint and spring onions, stale odour of kerosene fumes, and John's tobacco smoke. The living room had the quietness of a school after the children have left for home and there are only reminders of their presence: open books, posters on the walls. Here the magazines lay neatly stacked on the coffee table, a perfectly sharpened pencil and writing pad beside the telephone, a perfumed candle beside the window sill, a Bible and a hymn book next to the piano.

On the mantelpiece, was an envelope with Arun's name written boldly across it, marked with the usual flourish of Victoria's handwriting. She often left little messages on pieces of paper on top of the mantelpiece if she was not going to be there at mealtimes or when going out of town. Underneath the message she would write 'Have a blessed day' or 'Lots of love', and sign her name. Arun opened the envelope, hoping to find a note from Victoria, but to his surprise it was the cheque she had written for Mr Gupta.

He tiptoed to the kitchen and gave a cough so as not to startle John.

'Come in, Doctor Sahib. I heard you open the door,' said John. 'I am so glad to see you. Miss Sahib has not eaten well for the two days you were gone. God only knows what she will do once you leave in a couple of months.' He continued to polish the brass base of the kerosene stove with Brasso until he could see the engraving 'Primus Stoves' clearly.

'I am glad to be back from Chakrata. Are you trying to clean the stove?' asked Arun, stating the obvious.

'I am, Sahib. I have all the time in the world. The nearer I am to the house of God the more time I seem to have.' He was clearly having difficulty finding the kerosene jet outlet of the stove. He held a small, shiny aluminium strip with a fine needle at one end. John's tremulous hands could not possibly manoeuver the needle into the outlet. He had lost so much weight lately that the veins on his arms and forehead appeared like lush green ferns.

Arun wondered if John had told Victoria that he was dying. Or did she herself guess that he would not be around for too long? He was now a spent candle closer to its base, bathing in its flickering light, which was still undaunted and radiant.

John said, 'You should marry Nurse Miss Sahib. She came here in your absence and cried and cried. Victoria Miss Sahib was very upset, too.'

'John, I am too young to get married.'

'Too young, Sahib?' John laughed. 'One rarely comes at these crossroads in life. When a woman's gaze is full of questions for you and you only, you must not shy away. Who am I to tell you? If you marry young, you grow with your children; if you marry late, you grow old in front of your children. You must be hungry.'

'I am extremely hungry,' Arun admitted, as he bent over and took the aluminium strip from John's hand and cleaned the jet outlet of the stove. He pumped the plunger of the metallic stove to ignite the jet of kerosene that burst into a flame. The hiss of the flame gave life to the kitchen, and John's slow movements gained momentum as he stir-fried the fresh vegetables. Arun stood in the doorway watching John cook.

The thought of Trishna crying in front of Victoria irked him. Why did she have to do that? He wanted to get more information about the meeting but refrained from asking any more probing questions.

It was John who wanted to get something off his chest. 'Miss Sahib met a lawyer sahib, Mr Gupta, in the church on Sunday. She said you know him. He would like to come for the service next Sunday as well. She told me about the tragic death of his wife. Miss Sahib says he seems a very nice person,' said John, as he put the plate with piping hot stir-fried vegetables on the table.

'A lot seems to have happened since my trip to Chakrata.' Arun looked at the steaming vegetables, but his appetite seemed to have evaporated. He picked up the envelope and took out the cheque written to Mr Gupta. How strange that this very cheque lay in Mr Gupta's house for so long, and now he was holding it again; and how strange that this very cheque connected Mr Gupta to the woman who had become for Arun an anchor, a spiritual beacon, a symbol of indefinable love. Whenever Victoria gazed at Arun, she did not have any questions seeking answers, but only had answers for him.

'Why aren't you eating your food?' asked John.

'I am not hungry anymore.'

'Sahib, sudden loss of hunger only means jealousy.'

'Why do you say that John?'

'After all these years as a cook, I can usually tell a person's mood by the way they treat their food. I am not a doctor, but if you really want to know someone's character, just watch them eat. If you eat fast, it means something, and if you eat too slowly, it means something. When your hunger vanishes even when you were hungry a few seconds ago, it could mean jealousy.'

'John, I am not jealous.'

John bent over to pick up a napkin that had fallen on the floor. He looked at it wistfully as he folded it again and shook his head. He seemed to be remembering something.

'You are, Sahib. Let me tell you the story of the Swedish ambassador's wife who was my mentor many, many years ago. I don't know why I am remembering her today. God bless her, wherever she is.' John lit another cigarette. His lips caressed the cigarette end, his cheeks caving in as he inhaled deeply, making the mauve veins on his taut forehead a shade deeper.

'The ambassador was a handsome man, but his wife was rather plain. He loved to host parties at the embassy, where I saw many famous people, including Mrs Indira Gandhi's son, Sanjay. In one of those parties the ambassador met a very beautiful lady, a friend of Sanjay Gandhi, who could drink like a man. She had big eyes, and the ambassador had eyes only for her. The lady was well known to all the cooks in other embassies. She attended many parties, and we all thought she was a spy.'

'Was she really a spy?' asked Arun, looking interested.

John could tell his sulk was on the wane. 'Sahib, there was no doubt she was someone important.'

'Then what happened? Go on.'

'One day, when the ambassador's wife returned home after playing cards at the Gymkhana Club, she found the lady in her bedroom with her drunk husband. I had stir-fried some vegetables, but she did not eat anything that night—and for a few days after.'

'John, I do not have that kind of jealousy, you know that.'

'Yes, Doctor Sahib, not that kind of jealousy, but you are jealous of any friendship between Mr Gupta and Miss Sahib. I hope you will forgive me for saying this. You have to eat this food.'

'I will eat, John. Tell me, did the Swedish ambassador's wife keep in touch with you after you left Delhi?'

'No, Doctor Sahib, after some deal was done with the Army, the ambassador was transferred to his country. I do miss the ambassador's wife sometimes; she was a good lady. I was glad to get away from Chanakyapuri. I did not have any friends at the embassy anyway. The gardeners were very educated, unlike me, and I knew they were only pretending to be gardeners.'

There was a restful quietness to the afternoon: a gentle breeze in the banyan tree and the occasional outburst of a lonely cicada hiding in some tree bark as the two of them talked. John puffed his cigarette slowly, and Arun observed him smoking in the unrestrained stillness of the afternoon, musing on what John had accused him of. Maybe he was jealous of Mr Gupta being friendly with Victoria.

Arun finished eating the stir-fried vegetables, and he made sure that not a morsel, or even a stem, was left on his plate so as not to offend John. He then asked John, 'Do you think Victoria Memsahib will ever marry someone?'

John put out the cigarette and threw the butt into an

empty jam bottle. He smiled at Arun. 'I am sure she will one day. Maybe someone from here, or some gora sahib from England. I hope someone from here, so that she does not have to go back to England. She loves this place.'

Arun picked up the cheque and once again gazed at Victoria's signature. Strange that Mr Gupta never encashed the cheque after all the heartache he had caused, and he was still not sure what the Superintendent's intentions were regarding his certificate. A sudden sense of loss enveloped Arun. The thought of Mr Gupta coming to attend the Sunday service with Victoria seemed surreal, as if a demon had become a family friend.

As John went about washing the dishes, Arun sat staring at the cheque. He carefully folded it and left the envelope on the mantelpiece.

❖

That evening, Victoria had invited Reverend Phillips to join them for supper, partly to clear any misconceptions about Mr Gupta's sudden appearance at the mission compound. She was happy to see Arun back from Chakrata.

The Reverend sat rather stiffly at the dining table as Victoria told him about the tragic circumstances under which Mr Gupta's wife had perished. The Reverend patted his knuckles and listened intently, throwing an occasional nod in the direction of Arun, and then said, 'Oh, My Lord, that was so unfortunate. You knew her personally?'

'Yes, for a few months she was my colleague.'

Victoria passed the bowl of soup to the Reverend, who sat with the self-assuredness of a man who had lived on two continents. He spoke with nostalgia, beginning his sentences with 'In Canada' or 'When I was in Canada', as if he was not sure under which sky he was comfortable.

'So, you drove on a motorbike to Chakrata? So brave of you and your friend to ride in this kind of traffic.'

'It wasn't bad once we got out of Dehradun.'

'In Canada, the roads are so smooth and linear; they look like runways.'

Arun nodded, trying to imagine such roads.

'Would you like some more soup, Reverend?'

'Yes, Victoria, this is as delicious as the Canadian chowder.'

'You do miss Canada, don't you?' said Victoria, passing the soup.

'In some respects, yes, though I hated the cold weather.' He laughed.

17

The postman liked this season of the year. Every time he lugged a parcel from 'home', just before Christmas, Victoria gave him five rupees. Her family rarely sent her parcels now, but her dear friend, Sue, an aid worker with Oxfam, always sent her a gift no matter which part of the globe she was in.

This one was from England, with stamps of Her Majesty, and cellotape diagonally across the box, which reminded her of the Union Jack. Sue had sent her presents from Australia, Belize, Kenya and other far flung places where once the sun had lit the British Empire. At this time of the year, she missed the crowded streets of London the most; the aroma of colognes and perfumes from department stores like Debenhams and Selfridges, the sonorous strain of the engines of the red double-decker buses as they pulled into the stops to pick up old ladies in winter coats and hats.

Victoria carefully opened the parcel. There was the smell of England from the shredded packing of paper, almost like the wholesome smell of sealed air in a tin full of well-baked biscuits. She drew a breath and then her fingers felt the tops of bottles and an assortment of small packages. She took out the yellow-topped jar of Marmite and placed it on the dining table. There were bottles of marmalade from Marks and Spencer, bars of Pears and Imperial soap, face creams, and at the bottom, large bars of Cadbury's chocolate. God bless her heart, she thought.

She sat down near the window overlooking the garden and the banyan tree. The small table near the piano, where she kept her 'To Be Sent' tray, still had the card to her brother, Jack. He seemed always so engrossed in his life that he only remembered her once a year at Christmas time. He had led a rather measured life. He worked for the post office. He walked to work, whistling. Once a year he went to Majorca for holidays with his wife, and probably to the same hotel each year. He read *The Sun* and *The Mirror*. This year he had written a short note that detailed his wife's illness with breast cancer:

It has messed up my whole routine. I was looking forward to my retirement, the so-called golden years.

He had always seemed to have achieved a perfect balance between his wants and needs without the help of spirituality. She wondered whether she should remind him in her letter of the hope offered by Christ, or would he somehow balance his telescopic view of life despite his wife's illness.

This year, she did not feel excited about applying for a furlough to England. She usually spent a day at Jack's bungalow whenever she visited England, and then stayed at various dioceses in England and Wales, where she gave talks to awestruck parishioners about her work in the orphanage in Dehradun. A gentleman had once asked her, quite seriously, how far this Doon was from Timbuktu.

But there was something about 'home' at this time of the year that gnawed at her heart. It was the air of festivity, the politeness of the cashier ladies as they said 'Ta' and 'Thank you, my love' to strangers. The sound of church bells ringing and the commuter trains; the light rain, just enough to annoy but not enough to hinder walking; the smell of England in moisture-laden air and soot, and in the salt and vinegar on potato chips from the local chippy wafting through the narrow alleys of London.

Her moment of reverie was broken by the sound of the school bell, and she knew her girls would be dashing to the playground. She rummaged through the mail and found a pink envelope with neat handwriting that seemed faintly familiar. She opened the envelope and found a Christmas card from Mr Gupta. It read: *Wishing you a very merry Christmas and may peace be upon all of us. I look forward to the next church service.*

The words seemed to be strung from an invisible bar in perfect alignment, just as the bar over the Devanagari script.

Victoria wondered if Arun would be going away to see his uncle for the holidays. Deep in her heart she wished he would not go away, but really she couldn't blame him if he did. She began to plan a Christmas hamper for him. English chocolates would be a good start. Perhaps an aftershave or cologne, but then she remembered how the bees had attacked him after he put on the fruity aftershave his mother had sent from England. Perhaps, she could invite Trishna for Christmas dinner, then maybe not, because lately he had been a little too distant: no Scrabble for a long time, and weekend trips with his friends... Maybe all the attention Trishna was giving him was too overwhelming.

The last few months had gone by so quickly, and in another few months he would leave, and maybe she would never see him again.

Sometimes, like now when she was thinking of returning home, she wondered where was home? When she was young, just out of England and arriving in this foreign land, so different from the world of Rudyard Kipling and Rumer Godden, she had written to the Bishop in her exasperation: 'I wish to return home.' The Bishop had written back: 'Home is where you have Jesus with you, and He is everywhere, just look around you.' That sentence had changed the course of her life. She was still in India and felt blessed to be able to feel His presence.

John brought her a cup of tea and some English biscuits. He stood there after he had set the tray on the table. She looked up at him. 'Anything the matter, John?'

'Miss Sahib, I need some money.'

'How much do you need?'

'About hundred rupees to buy some groceries.'

'Why so much?'

'Miss Sahib, I want to make a Christmas cake, the best you may have ever eaten. This may be the last Christmas cake I will ever bake.' She lowered the cup of tea. When she looked at John in the eye, he noticed how blue her eyes were in the afternoon sun.

'Are you leaving me?'

'No, Miss Sahib, no, how could you think like this?' He poured her another cup of tea. 'Doctor Sahib says I have advanced lung cancer.'

Their silence was tainted by the sound of the silver spoon against the fine bone china and the tinkling of the little beads of the net covering the milk pot, as he poured the precise amount of milk into her tea. Then he stood upright with clasped hands, waiting for her to say something, but she was quiet as if in prayer. He waited.

'There is something more, Miss Sahib,' he continued after she had opened her moist eyes. 'Would you please take care of my daughter?'

She tilted her head ever so slightly, like those times when she had something important to say to her schoolgirls. He knew her subtle expressions and mannerisms, and whatever she was going to say, she would mean it. She parted her lips, and after a pause said: 'Indeed, Jesus is here. He is here; He will look after her.'

He did not understand what to make of her answer.

She warmed her toes in the shifting wintry sunlight of December, the so-called rosy warmth in India, which is more conducive to the glass jars of pickled mangoes placed on roof tops and porches to mature, and pondered over what John had said. 'Have you sought any treatment from the local hospital for your condition?'

'Yes, Miss Sahib,' he cleared his throat. 'They say my cancer can only be treated by x-rays in Delhi, but that will give me only a few more months.'

Victoria handed him a hundred-rupee note from her little purse. John made his customary obeisance and said: 'According to Ram Lal, the sweeper, there is some hope for me if I get certain plants from the Valley of Floors.'

'You mean Valley of Flowers?'

'Yes, Miss Sahib, the Valley of Floors where Hanumanji went to get the magic plants that brought Laxman back to life.'

She herself had dreamed of visiting the Valley of Flowers in the upper reaches of the Himalayas as a young girl after reading about Lady Joan Margaret Legge, the iconic botanist who fell to her death while collecting plants from there. Her solitary marble grave lies in the verdant garden of the fairies, fanned by icy winds and bears an inscription from the Bible:

I will lift mine eyes
Unto the hills
From whence cometh
My help.

Victoria turned to John and smiled, patted him on his back, and said: 'I might come with you and collect some flowers myself.'

18

The little church reverberated with hymns, and in between, the gusto with which Reverend Phillips delivered the Christmas sermon captivated Mr Gupta. What Reverend Phillips said was that we human beings are all sinners in some way or another. But there was hope if we believed in the Father, the Son and the Holy Ghost. Mr Gupta liked the positive attitude of Christianity and the premise that sinning was an inherent part of humanity. It somehow made him feel more human.

After the service, he chatted with other parishioners, and slowly made his way towards Miss Lambert, carefully avoiding Reverend Phillips, who was bent upon shaking every hand. The sky was a brilliant blue with wayward clouds that cast an occasional shadow on the church.

'Beautiful Sunday morning, Victoria,' said Mr Gupta, quickening his step towards the gate that led to her bungalow.

'Indeed, it is beautiful, but I don't like the chill wind. I hope you enjoyed the service.'

'Oh, of course, and I liked all the hymns. There is so much to be grateful for despite all the pitfalls of life.'

'Yes, indeed.'

He wanted to quote a hymn but could not remember the words. He opened the creaky and rusting iron gate for her.

'Thank you,' she said, lifting her skirt to avoid the brambles waving in the wind.

'Victoria,' he said, getting a little breathless keeping up with her brisk walk, 'I have a cheque for you—for your school rather.' He pulled a cheque from his jacket.

'Oh, my. That is very generous of you, Mr Gupta. Are you sure you want to give this huge amount?'

'Victoria,' he said, holding her soft hands. 'On the contrary, I wish I could do more in the memory of my wife.'

Reverend Phillip had followed them up to the litchi grove. When he saw Mr Gupta holding her hand, he quickly turned back towards the church.

'Would you like to come in and have some tea?' Victoria asked Mr Gupta.

'I would be delighted.' He loved the smell of her old English bungalow. The wooden floor exuded the scents of teak and coffee. There was the smell of old books, leather-bound Bibles, and fresh flowers on the dining table.

John appeared out of nowhere carrying two glasses of water on a tray as if he had been expecting them. 'You have a nice place here, Victoria. Don't you feel lonely in this big bungalow?' asked Mr Gupta.

'In India, one can be alone but never lonely. In Britain, one can be alone and lonely, if you know what I mean.'

'Yes, of course. And your work must keep you busy.'

'When you are in the service of God, one needs to be lonely, or should I say alone or both, to be in His presence.' She crossed her legs sideways and sat on the cane sofa. John laid the tea on the table. 'This must be a trying time for you, Mr Gupta,' she remarked, pouring the tea into his cup.

'I am coming to terms with it. Coming to your little church helps me a lot. Had I not brought back the cheque for Dr Arun, I would never have found your church—or solace.'

'Well, we have a service every evening. You are most welcome to join.'

He sipped the tea, which seemed a little insipid to him, but he felt compelled to say it was wonderful. Being an avid reader, his gaze fell upon her bookshelf that housed the works of Graham Greene, E.M. Forster, P.G. Wodehouse and John Masters. He felt calmed by her intellectual aura and hoped she would understand the burden he was carrying in his heart.

'Would you care for another cup of tea?'

'I would love to have another cup. May I ask you a personal question? What made you choose to become a missionary?'

She smiled at him and crossed her legs in the opposite direction. 'I did not choose to become a missionary. God chose me.'

'I have a confession to make to you. You see, my mother never liked my wife because she had always made choices for me. I was her only child, and after my abrupt love marriage, she somehow felt threatened about her motherhood.'

'But doesn't this sort of thing happen in most Indian households from what I understand?'

'By and large that is true. And they say an Indian man never grows up until his father dies, and it is only then that he learns to make independent decisions. There is something...' Mr Gupta stopped mid-sentence as John appeared again carrying another teapot. The Sunday afternoon seemed serene until the warm sunshine on the eucalyptus trees stirred the cicadas into a chorus with the mistaken portents of early spring.

'There is something weighing heavily upon my heart that I would like to share with you alone. You see, Dr Arun, your friend,' he paused looking around nervously and playing with his shirt button, almost whispering in a hoarse voice said, 'never lost my wife's wedding rings.'

'What do you mean?'

'Well, I hope you will not share this with anyone else. You see…all this time…my mother kept saying my wife had lost the wedding rings, but then, after the fire, I found them somewhere I never expected to find them.' Victoria looked at him intently and folded her arms across her chest, waiting expectantly. He had paused and buried his face, which she thought was quite handsome, in his large hands. 'They were in my mother's secret safe. And because of that—although it is hard for me to believe it—an awful thought comes to my head. Maybe the gas leak wasn't an accident, after all.' He took another sip of tea, which had gone cold. 'It is a terrible thought that haunts me.'

Victoria sat listening quietly. She considered reminding him there was more hot tea in the pot.

Looking at her bookshelf wistfully, Mr Gupta broke the silence. 'I see you read Graham Greene.'

'Yes, I do a lot of reading. It keeps me sane.'

'Isn't there a line in one of Greene's short stories… something like: "An open sin is only half a sin, and a secret innocence is only half innocent"?'

'Time will heal everything, Mr Gupta. I see that Christ is already showing you the way. Thank you so much for such a generous donation for the school.'

'It is my privilege. I shall see you at the church service next Sunday.'

19

There is something about Holi. It allows one to transcend all barriers of hierarchy, class, religion, colour—and, of course, friendly ribaldry, more often than not, is the norm. For a few hours one can throw colour on anyone, and everyone looks like an alien or visitor from a parallel universe of happy demons. For Victoria, Holi was one Indian festival that was decidedly pagan, and her only consolation was that Easter was just around the corner. She stayed indoors, fearful of the merrymakers who might appear at her gate.

Arun had left hurriedly for the hospital on his bicycle, where Sodi was busy rubbing pink-coloured powder on the cheeks of the graceful sweeper woman whom he admired every morning on his way to the wards. Rana appeared to be drunk. He stood near the main entrance of the hospital, surrounded by his friends from the local political party. He looked like a limp mushroom in the sun. A young kid threw a water-filled balloon, which burst like a ripe tomato on Rana's shirt. This drew laughter from the bevy of nurses on the balcony of the hospital. The splash of coloured water was a welcome relief from the triumphantly warm March winds that blew across the great Indian plain after the winter.

Arun wondered if he would see Sujata anytime today. It would have been too risky for her to drive through the bazaar on her scooter, an easy target for people with water guns on rooftops and balconies. Very little work would be done at the hospital, because even the patients seemed to have gone home or cancelled their surgeries. Sujata had promised to come to the hospital because she had something important to tell him.

He tried to look up at the balcony, squinting his eyes to see if Trishna was there. The sun was sharper and more brilliant at this time of the year. From the corner of his eye, he saw Trishna waving at him. When he waved back, the other nurses burst into applause, which made him uneasy.

Sodi walked towards him with a spring in his step. His face was painted bright pink and his beard was blue, which made him look like a sage of sorts. His confident smile was an indication that he had made some progress with the sweeper woman.

'Happy Holi, Arun!' he shouted, giving him a big hug and lifting him up.

'Happy Holi to you. Have you seen Sujata anywhere?'

'Sujata, of course. She is here somewhere. She was looking for you and—guess what?—we have been invited to her engagement party next week at the officer's club.'

'Engagement party?' Arun paused. With a slight tilt to his head, he said, 'Don't tell me it is Major Dhillon!'

'But, of course, my friend. Don't look so bewildered. Didn't you know?'

'I knew, I knew,' Arun stammered, 'that her mother never wanted her to marry an army man after what happened to her father.'

'Mothers and daughters only look alike, my friend,' said Sodi, putting his arm around him. 'They rarely think alike. How about some tea at Dallu's?'

'Sounds like a good idea.' As they walked through the

hospital compound, the sweeper woman gave Sodi a shy yet inviting smile. Arun quickened his step, leaving Sodi behind, his steps weighted by lingering looks.

At the tea shop, Dallu announced the first cup of tea would be free for everyone because of Holi. He poured hot tea into sturdy teacups. The festivities were almost over and the traffic on this busy road behind the hospital was down to a trickle.

'Sodi,' said Arun, 'why don't you find someone of... what shall I say...your own league?'

Sodi poured the steaming tea from his teacup into the saucer and took a big slurp. 'Relationships, my friend! See how you are looking for Sujata? I am afraid of relationships. You are into relationships; I am not. My fundamentals are clear. I am afraid of heartbreaks.'

'So how will you know the value of love if you haven't experienced heartbreaks?'

'You are senti, yaar! I will marry whomever my mother chooses for me. Besides, this is not the time for heartbreaks, it is time to look for a house job.'

'Have you applied already?' asked Arun, feeling a little left out.

'Applied? Heck no. You know how the system works in India. You need a pauaa, good connections, my friend. Rana will probably get a good hospital because of his political connections. I will end up in some military establishment, and you will end up going abroad. Sujata, well, she does not need a job; she will be a merry officer's wife.'

Sujata was busy distributing sweets to the nurses and patients in the ward. When she saw Arun, she ran up to him and unabashedly hugged him in the ward. 'Happy Holi!' she exclaimed.

'I hear there is some cause for celebration.'

'Oh, yes. I wanted to tell you first, but Major Dhillon told all the interns when he dropped me here. I came today to tell you about my engagement, otherwise I would not have come to the hospital on a day like this.'

'How is Vinod? Is he excited?'

'He is fine and so is my mother, believe it or not. Shall we go for a cup of tea at Dallu's?'

'I just had tea.'

'Oh, come on, another cup of tea won't kill you,' she cajoled him, entwining her arm around his.

The nurses looked on with what Arun thought might be envy as the two of them walked out of the ward, hand in hand. Knowing the warmth of her arm would be lost soon, all of a sudden, he unhooked his arm.

Dallu's tea shop was a shack made of bamboo, whose walls were made of khas-khas, which gave off an exotically sensuous smell in rain or sunshine. Dallu happily made tea all day in the enormous aluminium kettle that sat on hot coals. This shack was a sanctuary where glances were exchanged and sometimes hearts were broken.

'So what made you decide about Major Dhillon all of a sudden?' inquired Arun.

Sujata rested her face into the cup of her hands, pursed her lips and did not answer for a few seconds. 'Well...it was time for me to make some choices,' she said, playing with her teaspoon and then stirring her tea. 'You see, there is something to be said about staying put in a place, you know what I mean. Where I have grown up, where my blind brother has grown up. These roads and narrow lanes will change, but they will change with me.' She laughed. 'The only things that will never change will be the mountains you see from here. I don't think I could ever live in a foreign country and leave these mountains behind, Arun.'

She extended her arm and touched the top of his knuckles with her fingertips.

Arun looked at the blue mountains above the city's haze. He held her hand and said: 'I understand.'

'Really?'

'I sure do.'

'Promise me one thing. You will come to my engagement party at the officer's club?'

'Of course, I will,' he replied.

❖

The officer's club had all the glitterati of an elite club. The gentlemen held their wives' hands as they alighted from the vehicles. Uniformed men saluted them, their brass belt buckles glittering in the setting sun. The civilian guests wore ties and dress shirts. The steps leading into the main hall were draped with carpet, somewhat faded but still a brilliant red. The walls with earthy colours were adorned with portraits of various army men. General Manekshaw's portrait with his handlebar moustache made the portraits of his predecessors look less daunting. There were photographs of the colonial past: of Bengal Lancers on horseback, being led by their English officers; sepia photos of Englishmen in shorts standing languidly over the carcasses of fine leopards; and British memsahibs in long dresses, posing with their array of servants.

Arun, along with all the interns and some nurses, including Trishna, walked nervously to the wooden dance floor. Trishna stepped gingerly, trying to dampen the noise of her high heels as she moved towards the stage where Major Dhillon sat like a newly crowned king. Sujata smiled graciously, holding her mother's hand. Vinod sat impassively, wearing his dark glasses.

The officers sat or leaned at the bar as if tired after a long battle, holding their drinks steady. Everyone stood up as the Commandant walked in with his plump wife, who wore a shimmering necklace. The officers' wives chatted with each other, in the manner of military wives, so as not to offend those above them in the hierarchy. Soon the party was in full swing as officers and their wives took to the dance floor. The commandant and his radiant wife had downed a few drinks and drew an applause as they began to fox-trot across the floor. Arun, Sodi and Rana were back at the bar for a third round, but waited patiently for the officers to be served first. There was a rush of clicking heels and a sudden hush. The commandant's wife had fallen on the floor and lay in her husband's arms. Sodi and Arun rushed to the dance floor towards them, but the commandant raised an arm as if to hold them back. His wife's pale white ankle in gold high-heeled sandals lay twisted backwards. He lay her down and when he tried to unbuckle her sandal, she gave a shrill cry and passed out. 'Can somebody call the bloody ambulance!' He commanded. Major Dhillon let go of Sujata's waist to join a few other officers to carry the Commandant's wife off the dance floor. Military vehicles with flashing lights and an ambulance pulled up from the military hospital which was only few blocks away. The Commandant and Major Dhillon left with the entourage. The party had came to a standstill. When the susurrus of the military wives had died down, a senior officer requested the orchestra to play on.

Major Dhillon had been gone for some time. Trishna refused several young officers who asked her for a dance. Her eyes followed Arun, hoping to dance with him.

Sujata in her mermaid-like dress of sequins brought a Scotch for Arun. 'You know I don't drink whiskey,' he said.

'Well, you will have to drink it today.'

'Is that an order?'

'Indeed. It is my last day of freedom.'

Arun gulped the drink as though it were beer. Soon Sujata brought him another Scotch. He looked bleary eyed as she took a sip from his glass. 'Sujata, if I drink any more, I may say something we might regret.'

'Like what?'

The music by ABBA was too loud for the conversation. 'It is too loud and hot in here. Can't we walk outside?' she asked, taking another sip from his glass.

They slipped out from the back door. A full moon lit up the pond behind the officer's club, surrounded by tall grasses. A giant water tank, stilted on three supporting beams, looked like the fighting machine of the Martians from *War of the Worlds*. After walking a short distance on a path towards it, they sat under the tank behind the tall grass.

The music seemed distant. Only the bass sent vibrations which could be felt through the ground. They sat close together, and Arun put his arm around her waist. A soft breeze blew her hair to his lips. She flipped her hair back to the opposite side of her slender neck and kissed him with her whiskey-moistened lips. Then she began to undress quickly and shimmered in the opaque light like a naked Greek goddess by the water. It was so sudden that Arun became tongue-tied, as if a genie had appeared in front of him and he was too dumbfounded to make a wish.

Suddenly, the music got louder. Someone had opened the emergency back door. A shaft of light pierced through the swaying grass. Arun held her tightly and lay over her to cover her. A drunken officer staggered towards them. His footsteps came closer and closer until he stood almost above them. They both held their breath, aware of their thumping heartbeats. There was silence, and then a stream of hot urine somehow found Arun's ear hole and trickled down to his lips. He did not twitch a muscle. It seemed like an endless stream, and then a few drops, like the raindrops of a dying storm, sprayed his face. The officer zipped his trousers and sauntered back to the door.

'Do you think he saw us?'

'I don't think so. He was too drunk.'

'How did we get so carried away?'

'Maybe God was telling us something by sending that officer. It was my fault.'

'No, it was my fault as well. I feel so ashamed.'

'We have to go back fast and find out if he saw us.'

'But we didn't even see his face.'

'I don't think he saw ours, either.'

'How could I be so morally corrupt? So utterly insane to do this on my engagement day. You smell of urine,' she laughed.

They walked through the main entrance nonchalantly. It was Trishna who spotted them first. 'Where have you two been? Everyone is looking for you.'

'Just checking how long Major Dhillon will be at the military hospital.' Sujata smiled. 'Why don't you two dance while I take care of my mother?'

Arun's ear was still leaking the warm fluid; the stink began to make him feel dizzy. 'You sure look drunk!' said Trishna.

'I am not drunk, but now I know why they say "I am pissed". I need to use the gents,' he said, pointing to the shiny brass sign on the door.

Trishna was still waiting for him after he came out, looking as if he had had a bath. Meanwhile Major Dhillon had returned to a hero's welcome. The fellow officers raised him onto their shoulders and began to sing: *He is a jolly good fellow, he is a jolly good fellow...*

'They make such a good couple. You seem to look lost for some reason,' said Trishna, inching closer to Arun. The DJ put on an old Hindi song for the ring-exchanging ceremony, '*Haath aya hai jabse tere haath mein*'. Trishna was ecstatic. 'Oh, that is my favourite. It is such a romantic song. I don't know why you are looking so sad.'

'Why should I be sad on this happy occasion? I heard it may be your turn next to get engaged.'

'To whom?'

'Mr Gupta's cousin,' he teased.

'He likes me for sure, but that does not mean I am interested.'

Everyone was ordered to the dance floor. Arun and Trishna held hands and danced, while Sodi looked on from a distance and Rana slouched at the bar.

When Major Dhillon put the diamond ring on Sujata's finger, her expression changed. From then on, she only had eyes for Major Dhillon, and Arun was just a face in the crowd.

20

The valley was shrouded in a dusty haze, a sign that the first warm winds of summer were sweeping across from the plains and over the Shivalik hills and onto the ridge between the mountains. It was time for Mr Roy to take a break from the mundane government meetings at his post in Delhi...something called the Joint Secretary.

Being a devout Bengali Christian bachelor, he enjoyed Victoria's company whenever he could get away from Delhi to this quiet retreat in the missionary compound. He enjoyed playing Scrabble with her in the evenings, taking walks in the litchi grove, or discussing books he had read in the course of the year and the subtleties of the Bible and other religions. Every year he made a substantial donation to the school.

He had the face of a benevolent monk, with arched eyebrows and Fred Astaire-style shiny black hair parted in the middle. He always carried a black briefcase, as if protecting some secret government dossiers.

Mrs Gandhi's Congress Party was in disarray. The sterilization programme was in full swing, and over eight million men and women had been sterilized. Mr Roy, a top bureaucrat in the health ministry, dealt with orders from the Health Minister, who in turn received orders directly from Sanjay Gandhi. The memory of the bulldozers at the Turkman Gate, like giant yellow grasshoppers devouring everything in their path to clear the slums, was still fresh. The acrid smell of burning plastic, rubber slippers, discarded tires and other bric-a-brac that may adorn a slum assaulted him again and again. Many young Muslims who resisted the demolition were forcibly sterilized. Although he had played no role in the incident, his department was in the direct chain of command.

This respite in Dehradun was much needed for his sanity. His chauffer drove him in a government car, a white Ambassador, which sped quietly out of Delhi on a two-way highway through the sugarcane fields of Uttar Pradesh, which were dotted with brick kilns. Sitting at the back of the car, he made charcoal sketches of the landscape that whizzed past him.

When his car pulled up on the gravel pathway to the compound, a young man was walking back from the hospital. Mr Roy lowered the window of his car. 'I am Mr Roy. Are you the young man Miss Lambert has been writing so much about?'

'I am Arun, Sir.'

'I have heard so much about you. Maybe I'll see you at supper time. Seven o'clock sharp. She is so particular about timings, isn't she?' He smiled and waved as he rolled up the window.

❖

That evening at the dinner table, Miss Lambert asked Mr Roy to say the Grace. He began with the Lord's Prayer: 'Our Father who art in Heaven, hallowed be thy name…' He closed his eyes and his serene voice became softer towards the end of the prayer.

'I hope you had a pleasant drive from Delhi?' asked Miss Lambert.

'The traffic seems to get worse every time I come here. There are more and more people. Do you know in the next twenty years the population of India will double unless we do something about it?'

Miss Lambert put her hand to her mouth and whispered, 'But I don't like the way it is being done.'

Mr Roy gave an involuntary short laugh and his coffee-coloured Bengali complexion struggled to suppress a blush. He stirred the fresh tomato soup with his spoon thoughtfully. 'I could not agree with you more after witnessing the aftermath at Turkman Gate. And it is not just Turkman Gate.'

'Oh, Arun will tell you how he nearly became a statistic.'

'Oh, really?' said Mr Roy looking at Arun.

'I got off from a bus when the traffic light was red. The policeman caught me and took me to a nearby sterilization camp. Luckily, one of the hospital employees recognized me and I was let off.'

'That was a narrow escape indeed,' said Miss Lambert with a wink.

'So let me ask you this,' said Mr Roy, 'knowing the fact that we add the population of Australia each year to our population, how would you control it?'

'Through better education and opportunities for the people,' said Arun.

'Well, I am impressed, Dr Arun. What are your plans for the future?'

'I am applying for house jobs, but no interviews so far. There are too many candidates for so few training jobs. Many of my classmates will end up leaving the country.'

Over a meal of fish curry and rice especially prepared for Mr Roy, the three of them chatted into the evening. 'It is a shame, really,' said Miss Lambert, passing the rice to Mr Roy, 'when the country desperately needs trained doctors.'

Mr Roy rested his elbow on the table and raised his finger. 'If I may say, Victoria, our doctors don't want to work in rural areas, and there are good reasons for that, but

India spends ten lakhs per medical student. The education is almost free, and what we get in return is brain drain.'

'Well, can you help Arun stay in India? He has more than one reason to emigrate to the UK. You know how things work in India. It is who you know and not who you are.'

'Well, I will try my best to help this young man. At least in India everyone knows someone. I don't know about the UK.' It was Miss Lambert who blushed this time.

Their conversation was interrupted by a phone call from Delhi for Mr Roy. He spoke in a subdued voice as he said 'Yes sir! Yes sir!' Little diamonds of sweat appeared across his forehead.

'I'm afraid my sojourn in Dehradun has been cut short by a crisis in Delhi. I've been summoned back to the capital. I shall have to leave on Sunday morning and will miss the morning service at the church,' said Mr Roy apologetically.

The following morning Mr Roy's chauffer was adding the finishing touches to polishing the car. He stood to attention and saluted Mr Roy as he walked towards the bungalow. John had already laid the table for breakfast. Arun was waiting for Victoria when Mr Roy arrived.

'I have this letter for you to take to the Superintendent of a hospital I think will be suitable for you. I wish you good luck for the job. My apologies to Miss Lambert, as I shan't be staying for breakfast. Would you be kind enough to ask John to prepare some boiled egg sandwiches for me?'

'I shall bring them over to you, Sir,' said Arun, taking the letter, 'I don't know how to thank you.'

The morning sun disappeared behind dark grey clouds. The wind suddenly subsided, and there was a distant rumble, followed by the strike of the first hailstone on the tin roof.

Mr Roy stood up and said, 'It looks like I am heading into a storm—literally.'

21

It was the month of March. By mid-morning the Delhi sun was beating relentlessly on the concrete building of the hospital. The hot air lay densely in the corridor facing the Superintendent's office, and nothing stirred except a solitary fly, which added to the frustrating wait for Arun.

The air conditioner jutting out from the office window was blowing warm air suffused with the smell of fried onions, no doubt from the many tiffins of home-cooked food. The clerical peon in khakis, smoking an acrid bidi, sucked in his cheeks and seemed to swallow the smoke rather than inhale it. He had an expression of earned boredom—that of a crocodile after a large meal. Arun had been waiting for almost two hours, clutching the letter from Mr Roy for the Superintendent. He mustered enough courage and asked the peon, 'Could you let the Superintendent Sahib know I would like to see him?'

The peon flicked the bidi and said: 'He is in a meeting. I have told you for the third time.'

In reply, Arun elevated the status of the peon to big brother: 'Bhai Sahib, surely the meeting cannot last for two hours. I have travelled all the way from Dehradun to see him.'

The man threw the bidi into the corridor with a contemptuous look and stamped it with a slow twist of his leg. 'Arre bhai,' he said, 'people come from all corners of

India to get a job, but first they have to see me. Perhaps it is difficult for you to understand,' he laughed. 'In this hot weather one needs chai-pani.'

Arun understood exactly what he meant by chai-pani, but he was in no mood to part with his hard-earned money. He moved to the bench outside the Superintendent's office. He buried his head in his hands and sat cross-legged on the bench.

After an hour, the peon lost his patience and tapped on Arun's shoulder to wake him up. 'You can go in now,' he said abruptly.

The first thing that hit him was the cool air of the office. There was at least a 30-degree temperature drop from the outside world. The hair on his forearm stood up. The Superintendent, a fair man with a shock of white hair, invited him to sit down. Arun felt goose pimples springing up all over his body.

'Sir, I would like to do a surgical house job at your prestigious hospital. I have brought my CV for you.' His throat was getting dry, but with some effort, he was able to mumble, 'And this letter from Mr Roy.'

The Superintendent grabbed the letter from his hand and quickly skimmed over it. 'Yes, he called me a few days ago. When do you finish your internship?'

'At the end of this month, Sir.'

'I am sure you are aware how competitive it is to get into this hospital. Why did you choose to do your internship at this obscure place—Dehradun?'

Arun cleared his throat, and after taking a deep breath he blurted, 'Sir, I wanted to work in a place and at a hospital that represents the rest of India.'

'Very good, very good. I am sure you had good experience for what it is worth. The list will be out in three weeks. Congratulations, and now you may leave.'

'Thank you, Sir,' Arun stammered and hesitated for a while, doubting if he had heard the word 'congratulations' correctly. He closed the door carefully behind him and walked into the dazzling midday sun. Another young man, roughly of his age, was sitting on the bench. He wore well-creased shiny trousers and seemed to be joking with the peon, who was handing him a cup of tea. 'How was the interview? What did he ask you?' the young man asked him excitedly.

'He asked me where I had trained.'

'Where did you train?' asked the young man.

'Dehradun.'

'That is in UP.'

'Where did you train?' asked Arun.

'Delhi. Brother, It is easy to get into this place if your father is a government employee.'

'Is your father a government employee?' asked Arun nervously.

'Sort of, he is a member of the Parliament.'

'Good luck, brother,' said Arun as he hurried away.

22

A few miles from the hospital an extraordinary event, the kind that would change destinies, was taking place at the Ramlila Grounds. The jacaranda trees lining the roads named for the ghosts of the Mughal and British empires, like Bahadur Shah Zafar Marg and Curzon Road, were in full bloom. Mrs Gandhi had declared general elections after lifting the Emergency rule, and the opposition had gathered at Ramlila Grounds. Mr Jagjeevan Ram, once a confidante of Mrs Gandhi and a minister in her cabinet, had defected to the opposition. He was one of the few surviving freedom fighters. He wore Gandhian clothes and a white cap which accentuated his dark complexion. His prominent lips, despite his short stature, gave him an air of authority. After a rousing speech for democracy, he complained of some chest pain. An ambulance hemmed in by police vans and white Ambassadors rolled into the hospital from the grounds. All roads were blocked.

A few streets from the hospital, Mrs Gandhi's aides were briefing her on the situation. His defection and campaign for the opposition could severely challenge her re-election. She called the Health Minister and asked him if he could do anything to extend Mr Jagjeevan Ram's stay at the hospital.

'Madam, hospitals are peculiar places. Sometimes it can be made difficult to discharge patients hurriedly. I will contact the appropriate doctors and ensure he gets a full check-up,' the Health Minister assured her.

Later in the day, the Health Minister summoned Mr Roy to his office. 'Mr Roy, you must be aware, the Honourable Mr Jagjeevan Ram was taken to one of our finest hospitals. It is imperative that we give him the best medical care and bring him back to health. His campaign should come second, his health is most important to our Prime Minister. Perhaps he should recuperate in the hospital until the elections are over. Call the Superintendent for a meeting with you and update me with the situation.'

Mr Roy shook his head a few times. Out of respect, he looked towards the minister's nose rather than his eyes, which reminded him of an inverted Nepali kukri, and said, 'Understood, Sir, yes, Sir. Yes, Sir.'

Mr Roy wasted no time. The Superintendent was informed to do the needful, as they say in government circles. The treating physician, a cardiologist, was honoured to be the chosen one. It would open so many avenues for him. Little did he know that he was a mere puppet in the hands of the Prime Minister.

❖

That evening, as the honourable politician lay on the hospital bed surrounded by his concerned party members, the cardiologist politely asked them to step outside. He took Mr Jagjeevan Ram's hand in his and noticed how warm it was. Then, in a soft voice he said: 'Sir, I have some news for you that is not good. I think this election campaign has taken a toll on your health, and I think you have suffered a heart attack.' He unfurled a roll of EKG tracing and pointed to peaked ST waves. Then the cardiologist played with the stethoscope nervously, knowing the EKG belonged to someone else.

Mr Ram turned a little pale and moistened his lips.

'Sir, you need not worry about anything. You are in

good hands, and I will order all the procedures needed. Perhaps you should keep this information to yourself and close family members, as people can take advantage of the situation. One thing I must emphasize is that you need a lot of rest.'

'But, Doctor, you know I am in the middle of my campaign.'

'Sir, rest is essential for your complete recovery.'

The Superintendent informed Mr Roy that everything was under control. There were a lot of visitors at the hospital but the Superintendent kept the press at bay as far as he could; however, the news of the heart attack had somehow leaked to the press.

❖

A young MD student working for his thesis under the cardiologist was not convinced about the heart attack. The subsequent EKGs somehow did not match the original EKG. There seemed to be a dramatic difference. Could his boss have made a mistake? During the morning round, he asked the cardiologist, 'Sir, the initial EKG had a right bundle branch block as well, which is missing in the later EKGs. I wonder if the EKG shown to you…'

The cardiologist cut him short. 'As an MD student you are always concerned about the minutiae. You should always look at things clinically. Forget about the EKG. You should concentrate on your thesis and about getting an MD.'

'Sir, my thesis is on the aberrations of EKGs, that is why I find it so interesting.'

The cardiologist felt somewhat irked by this upstart. He agitatedly rotated the stethoscope suspended from his neck. The MD student knew his boss was clearly flustered from the way he was rotating his stethoscope in circles.

'I want to handle everything personally as far as Mr Jagjeevan Ram is concerned. Didn't you say you wanted leave to get married?'

'Yes, Sir,' answered the student, with a look of disbelief.

'You may take a couple of weeks off,' he said, grabbing Mr Jagjeevan Ram's chart from the younger man's hand.

The student walked to the canteen, feeling the barbs of rebuke. Why was the boss so defensive about Jagjeevan Ram? Sitting at the table, he found Dr Hussaini, an arch rival of his boss. He was one of the few foreign-returned doctors who had returned with a British wife and the coveted MRCP from London from the Royal College in the UK. He annoyed the home-grown, never-out-of-the-country doctors with words like bloke and chaps, and wore a bowtie instead of a tie.

'I agree this chap's EKG does not match Mr Jagjeevan Ram's EKG. Interesting! So very interesting!'

No one will ever know who leaked the story to the press. There were conspiracy theories that somehow the Government was involved in keeping Mr Ram in the hospital. The Government, of course, denied it had anything to do with it. Mrs Gandhi had, in fact, called Mr Ram and wished him a speedy recovery. The Health Minister promised to look into the integrity of the doctor concerned.

Mr Roy was quietly transferred to the state of Bihar, a backwater of the country, as Secretary to the Minister for Posts and Telegraphs. The new Health Minister of the country was Mr Raj Narain, a maverick of sorts who rode on a bicycle to attend cabinet meetings. Mr Ram successfully campaigned under the banner of the party he had founded, Congress for Democracy. The Janata Party won 274 seats with the help of Mr Ram's party; the alliance had shifted the balance of power in seismic proportions to dethrone the Empress, the Razia of India, the invincible Mrs Indira Gandhi.

❖

Three weeks later, Victoria had a prayer service at the church to wish Arun good luck for his house job in Delhi. He was nervous about the list of successful candidates to be posted. He felt his name would probably be on the top since it began with an 'A'. He hoped to see Mr Roy personally to thank him.

As the bus cut through the Shivalik hills, he felt exposed to the expanse of the gigantic plains ahead and the new life that awaited him. He had received a letter from his mother in England. He did not want to read it on the bus just yet. He had also bought two newspapers, which sat unread on his lap.

The year had gone by so quickly. The villages he saw from the window of the slow-moving bus seemed timeless and oblivious to the change that was taking place in the country. Cows waddled in village ponds, surrounded by lush green fields; young girls tended the livestock as the sun beat down upon their dark skin. Brick hutments with narrow alleys disappeared over the hillocks; and then more fields and dried-up riverbeds passed by, and then another village just like the one before. He wondered what the villagers did if anyone got a toothache or appendicitis in the middle of the night. Here, nothing had changed since Independence.

He opened the letter from his mother. Her letters always started with 'How are you' and 'We are well'. After the mundane sentences, she gently got into the details. His father had left the house and was no longer living with them. The only reason she gave was that perhaps it was too much for his father to suddenly cope with his teenage children, who had joined him after several years, and whom he had imagined as the little ones he had left in India. They were suddenly so grown up and rebellious. But Arun knew there would be more reasons. She talked about working in a 'factory'.

He leaned against the window and closed his eyes to the outside world. A tear made its way into his nostril. A fellow passenger picked up his newspaper, thinking he was asleep, and started reading it without asking him. He did not care.

There was a big crowd outside the Superintendent's office. Young men and women jostled to reach the notice board. Some were jumping with joy and others stood idly. Arun inched his way to the front. He started to read the names from the bottom up for some reason. He did not recognize any of the names, and then his heart began to pump wildly as he came to the names starting with A. He had reached the top yet he did not see his name. This time he read the names from the top of the list one by one. Soon he had reached the B column. How could that be? The Superintendent had promised him a house job.

The crowd began to thin. He spotted the young man in the shiny trousers whom he had seen on the day of his interview. 'Brother, I got into the surgical house job. How about you?'

'I wasn't so lucky, brother,' he said dejectedly.

There was no peon around this time when Arun knocked at the Superintendent's office door, which was half ajar. 'Come in,' said the voice inside. The Superintendent was taking down his diplomas and degrees. His desk looked empty.

'Sir, I am Arun, Mr Roy's friend. My name is not on the list.'

The Superintendent blew the dust off the jacket of one of

the books he had taken down from the bookshelf. 'Young man, the government has changed, and there are new masters with new lists. I am no longer the Superintendent,' he said, putting his book on the table and taking a deep breath. 'In this game, son, sometimes you win, sometimes you lose. You will win some other time.'

Arun looked at him as if he were looking at a magician whose trick had been suddenly exposed, or like a fallen god, a god without powers gathering his paraphernalia of lost command. 'Thank you for your advice, Sir,' he said and made his way to the door.

Now there was no crowd outside. The white dome of a gurudwara with its golden top glistened in the distance. He felt lost, and unable to think. He walked towards the gurudwara. A fortune-teller sat cross-legged on the marble steps. He seemed very fair, with blue eyes. At first Arun thought he was an albino, but after exchanging a few sentences in Hindi, it was clear he was an Englishman.

Putting his hand out, Arun asked, 'So, what do you see in my hand?'

'Close your fist and then open it.' He paused, and with a smile said, 'I see a lot of travel lines.'

'But don't we all have these lines?'

'Yes, we do. But only few people know how to use them.'

'So you mean I can make my own destiny?'

'Precisely,' said the Englishman.

❖

Arun made his way to the interstate bus station at Kashmere Gate, where the buses were parked chaotically. The night bus was already full of people. The bus station, although recently constructed, was an ugly structure of concrete beams splattered with posters. Strangely, graffiti was rather alien to the naked Indian walls, barring some warning signs like 'Urination Is Strictly Prohibited', but no wall was spared the indignity of being left uncovered by posters.

The only seating left was the bench at the back of the bus. Diesel smoke, human sweat and wafts of urine pervaded the bus. As soon as the ramparts of the city were left behind and the unauthorized colonies gave way to the fields of sugarcane, the Grand Trunk Road, lined with trees from the time of the Mughal Empire, stretched under the silvery moonlight, until it came to a railway crossing. The driver switched off the engine, and the bus seemed deathly quiet except for the occasional snore. Then the railway tracks lit up from the distant headlight of the steam engine.

The earth shook as the solitary cylindrical steam engine rolled across the landscape, breathing the night air with Herculean force and then disappearing like a dark shadow into nothingness. As the driver waited patiently for the night watchman to crank open the gates, Arun realized that this point in his life was just a pause, like the railway crossing. He had to wait patiently to find the tracks that lay in the darkness.

❖

The bus pulled into the terminal in Dehradun early in the morning. Shop fronts were still shut, and milkmen were getting on their bicycles. Stray dogs lay curled up in corners. The clamour hadn't started.

Trishna was waiting for him at the terminal. In the distance, the mountains were lit up by the first rays of the sunrise. Squinting her eyes, she spotted him at the back of the bus. As he got out, she said, 'Welcome home,' and smiled and hugged him.

'You smell nice,' said Arun.

'It's my sandalwood soap, made from no animal fat, pure vegetarian oils. Tell me, did you get the job?'

'No. My name was not on the list.'

'I thought Mr Roy was supposed to help you.'

'It is a peculiar story. I will tell you later.'

'Maybe God is telling you to settle down in Dehradun. I can help you set up your practice,' she offered, holding his hand.

He did not know what plans God had for him. There was so much more to learn in medicine. The memory of Dr Gupta haunted his dreams. Had she not misplaced her wedding rings, she would have been alive. Do our footsteps find the paths that led us to the oases and mirages in the desert, or do these paths find our footsteps?

'My family needs me in UK more than ever before. I do not think I can stay here,' he told her.

She picked up the end of her scarf and covered her face. 'I will wait for you. I know you will not like UK. You love the mountains; these mountains are your very own. Besides, do you not love me?' She sobbed into her scarf.

He put his arms around her, his face resting on her neck. The aroma of sandalwood calmed him. He closed his eyes and felt the pulsating blood vessels of her neck against his cheeks. 'Perhaps you can come to UK. They need nurses more than doctors.'

'You haven't answered me.'

'I wish I knew the answer.'

They reached the missionary compound. The litchi trees were laden with goose-pimpled reddish-purple fruit, just as he had first seen the compound almost a year ago. He did not see the bees that had chased him into the bungalow, or any bees for that matter. Instead, the yellow butterflies flew like kites on a summer's day. He had lived in this bungalow for almost a year. He knew the footpaths that crisscrossed the litchi grove to the bungalow. The wild rabbit had learned to ignore the vibrations of human feet and stood confidently on his hill. It was a node in Arun's life when he felt he was suddenly staring at the past while standing in the present. It was like leaving home for the first time, or saying goodbye for the last time, but with a false anticipation of reunion. He imagined seeing what was before him becoming a reality, a kind of postcard etched in his memory. Perhaps Victoria would leave for her home country in a year or two and no one would ever know who had lived here.

Under the canopy of fruit trees, Trishna stopped, turned around and faced him. 'How can you not know the answer to my question? Do you remember I went home for a few weeks when I first met you?'

'Yes, I do,' he said, putting his arms around her waist.

She pushed him away. 'I had gone away for a reason,' she said. Her eyes welled up to wet her long eyelashes, 'I think you should know. I was...I was...' she paused, her throat pulsating, and then she seemed to swallow her words 'well, I was pregnant... it is over.'

'What are you trying to tell me?'

Her voice had that cadence and control that comes with underlying deep regret, as if she'd been told about some terrible ailment. 'Do you remember what Bhag Singh once said to us? Perhaps you don't even remember him.'

'Of course, I remember Bhag Singh.'

'Well, he told us his child was God's gift. It could have been a God's gift for us, but I...' Her neck veins quivered with a sudden rush of blood. 'All this time my heart was heavy.'

The shade of the trees seemed cooler, and for a few moments, there was stillness, until his heart began to race as he tried to comprehend what she had told him. 'Why didn't you tell me all this at that time?'

She pulled him closer to her and said, 'Would you have believed me? It was not the right time for us.' Her eyes reflected a woman's regret in its multitudes, and then her face turned into anger. 'How could you dance with Sujata, tell me? She may be a doctor, but I have another word for her.'

'Let us not talk about Sujata. She is engaged as you know.'

'Yes, but you still have feelings for her,' she said in a husky voice.

'I hope you will never talk to Victoria about this.'

'How can I? I have done the most un-Christian act. I wake up in the middle of the night, every night, consumed by my guilt, which I was carrying alone.'

The morning school bell rang with its familiar echo. There was the distant collective chatter of schoolgirls walking to the school behind the woods. Early rays of the sun knitted through the tall eucalyptus trees around the missionary compound. The bungalow stood in the middle ground. He stared at the drops of moisture from its gutters, little pearls falling to the ground hesitatingly. Time stood still.

'I wish you had never told me anything,' said Arun in a soft voice.

'I cannot believe how you can be such a coward. What is done is done,' her voice decisive and piercing. 'You must now think about the future.'

As they walked towards the bungalow, Arun noticed a young boy behind the kitchen door eyeing them shyly, and then he disappeared. 'Who was that boy I just saw?'

'He is Ramu, Mr Gupta's old teenage servant. Don't you know Mr Gupta brought him to Victoria for work, but she would have none of it? She told him the young boy should be in school. He can help John, and she will pay for his school fees. One less servant in this land, don't you think?'

'That is wonderful,' said Arun. 'Would you ever keep a servant in your house?'

Trishna gave him a scornful smile. 'Never!' she said, her hair flying in the wind, and her silk sari hugging her contours tightly. 'Never, ever! All of the working women rely on servants. Their husbands have probably never eaten a meal cooked by their wives...chee! They are doomed to eat the food cooked by servants for the rest of their lives. That is what will happen if you marry one of that lot.'

Victoria must have heard their voices. She opened the front door. Like an angel, she lifted her arms and said, 'My, my, look who's here. Welcome back home. What is the news?'

Arun gave her a big hug and said, 'I did not get the job.'

23

Victoria busied herself with her daily chores, her mind preoccupied with the thought of staying alone once again in the bungalow. In a matter of days Arun would leave, to continue his journey to a new world. She dusted her bookcases and wiped her Bibles with a wet cloth. She picked the gladioli from her garden, taking her time, and made artistic arrangements with the ferns from the nearby stream, which lay hidden at the bottom of the hill. It was her private retreat where, under the green shade of the trees, she listened to the water rushing over the smooth, rounded stones. Here, as she closed her eyes, she transported herself to the brooks of Betws-y-Coed in North Wales where she had been sent as a child to escape the bombing of London during World War II. There was the same smell of damp earth, wet leaves, luxuriously green ferns and moss clinging to the boulders.

She had recited Psalm 23 to herself whenever she had felt lonely. She had read the psalm to Arun after Dr Gupta's death, and it gave him the much-needed solace to overcome his presumed guilt. She had the satisfaction of having introduced him to the love of Christ, and now it was his choice to accept Him as his saviour.

Lately, she had been thinking of giving a gift of sorts, something Arun would cherish forever and would remind him of the time he had spent at the mission compound. She knew how he would feel in a foreign land once the first flash of awe began to fade. There would be loneliness not only for the people he had known but for his very being, his soul, unless he had the Lord in his heart. Psalm 23, written and framed in her handwriting, would be the most appropriate gift. She feared the dazzle of the West would corrupt him into materialistic pursuits. He would forget what he was leaving behind.

At dinner, after Grace, she said, 'So you have decided to leave for London as early as next week?'

'I have no choice now. The date for the qualifying exam is the 15th of December in London. After I pass the exam, I can get a job in the National Health Service,' he said with new optimism.

She carefully unfolded the napkin and picked up her knife and fork. She noticed John had made roasted quails, one of Arun's favourite dishes. She cleared her throat. 'Of course, it will be very good for your family. I just wonder how the materialistic life of Britain will affect you.'

Arun looked puzzled. 'What do you mean by materialistic?'

'Well, you don't know how people in the West want more than they need. It is a disproportionate striving for one's wants.'

'I honestly don't understand what materialistic means. Want is an inner need. If you have it, then you need it.'

Victoria laughed. 'You are talking like a psychiatrist. It is not as simple as that. Perhaps, you will understand what I mean if I read Hebrew 13:5 to you.' She picked up the Bible with a deep blue cover embossed in gold letters. She read to him: *Let your conversation be without covetousness, and be content with things ye have: for He hath said, I will never leave thee, nor forsake thee.*

He did not understand what she was trying to tell him. She knew he did not understand the deeper meaning of life. She was not sure if he was leaving to help his family, or if his quest was for further knowledge of medicine. Would he return to help his country, where there was only one doctor for every three thousand people, or would he succumb to the so-called comforts of the West?

After she had finished reading, she asked him a question that seemed to startle him, and his nostrils twitched as if pulled by a rein. 'Have you thought about any long-term plans regarding Trishna?'

That very moment he surmised, perhaps Trishna had said something to her. He seemed to have blushed and could feel the blood rushing to his face, as he thought of what to say to her.

'Trishna really cares for you. She really does. It will be a shame if you lose her,' she said passing him the pineapple cake.

He fumbled with his plate and nearly dropped it. 'Well, I haven't given much thought to it really, as I have been so busy trying to get a house job. I cannot think of anything right now.'

'I understand what you mean. The Lord will guide you.'

After dinner, she told him she would be out of town for a few days. It was time to see the Bishop in Nagpur to seek another extension for her stay in Dehradun.

'You have a big day tomorrow, don't you, with the Superintendent? I hope she does not make too much fuss about your certificate. Although I don't think she will. Mr Gupta, bless his heart, has put in a good word for you.'

After Arun left she switched on her radio to listen to the BBC World Service. The news was depressing. Another prostitute had been murdered in the Midlands. There were strikes everywhere. The Leyland workers were demanding more pay, the police were demanding more pay, and the firefighters were on strike. What on earth is happening to Britain? she wondered. The country seemed to be in shambles, with soaring unemployment, increased crime rates and loss of moral values. Then there was Enoch Powell making inflammatory speeches about immigrants. This was not the country she had once lived in, and Arun would be heading into a morass of improbabilities. It was the sonorous voice of Malcolm Muggeridge with his weekly dispatches, 'Letter from America', heard around midnight, which helped her to go to sleep. The chimes of Big Ben, at the end of the program, reassured her and she felt at home, dozing off to sleep with the radio on.

❖

The interns were already standing outside the Superintendent's office by the time Arun reached the hospital. Sodi stood there, towering above the rest, adjusting his turban. Rana was fidgeting and had a broad smile. Sujata was nowhere to be seen.

Rana walked towards Arun and said, 'Have you heard the news?'

'No, what news? Is the Superintendent dead?' asked Arun facetiously.

'No, yaar, Indira Gandhi has been sent to jail. And I have landed a job with the CGHS in Garhwal.'

'So, what has made you happier?'

Rana gave a sheepish grin.

Sodi was pleased he was accepted into MD in Pathology in one of the Army hospitals. 'Can't deal with living things,' he said, 'even dead things scare me. I guess it wouldn't be bad in the Army. I will probably see a lot of cirrhotic livers.'

Everyone had a job lined up. Arun was the odd one

out. His name was called and he was the first to go into the Superintendent's office. The office was in disarray. Mrs Gandhi's portrait had been taken down and replaced with the edentulous smile of the Father of the Nation, Mahatma Gandhi. The Superintendent moved rather slowly towards Arun, holding his unsigned completion certificate.

'Sit down, Arun,' she said, sending his heart pounding as he noticed she had dropped the title doctor. 'You have been a good boy, I must say, from the reports I have received. I am very saddened we lost Dr Gupta,' her voice crackling. 'I misjudged you. Mr Gupta told me some time back he found his wedding rings in a strange place. A very strange place, indeed.' She picked up her pen and signed the certificate. As she handed it to him, she said wistfully, 'As the *Gita* says, what we see does not exist, what exists we fail to see.'

'Thank you, Madam,' he said, thinking ogres may not be what they seem.

It would be his last day in the hospital. New interns were pacing nervously in the corridors. Sujata had not come to pick up her certificate. She might be in one of the wards. He climbed the stairs to the second floor facing the main road. There was no sign of Sujata. The sun was streaming into the verandah, which had been turned into a medical floor. In one of the beds, a strange face stood out. He had blond hair and ruddy sun burnt white skin.

As Arun passed his bed, the patient unclenched the fingers of his left hand and beckoned him closer. He was an elderly man with long sinewy limbs that seemed a size too big for the medical bed. His restless blue eyes were set in a once-handsome face that reminded Arun of Rock Hudson's.

The man tried to pick up his right hand with his left hand. 'I cannot move the right half of my body, my boy. Damn!' he said, banging his left fist against the bed rail. His eyes moistened as he repeated his gesture.

Arun sat at the end of the bed and held his hand. 'When did this happen?'

'Two days ago. Wham! Just like that, my boy. Luckily, I was in the club and they rushed me here,' he said in his Anglo-Indian accent. 'I cannot believe there is no power in this arm or leg. I would like to share with you the strange dreams I have been having since my stroke. It is not about my wife whom I lost six months ago. It is of my younger days.'

'Tell me more. Go on.'

'Well, my boy, this is before you were born. When the Japs invaded Burma, I flew Hunter hurricane bombers from Assam. Last night, I dreamt I was flying a bomber over Burma. I could see the golden pagodas rising from the forests, shrouded in the morning mist. I bombed the bloody Japs with this very hand I cannot now move. Once, these hands released real bombs. I am sorry to take so much of your time, tell me if I will ever be able to walk?'

'It is going to take time, surely you will if you are determined,' said Arun, releasing the grip of his hand.

'These very hands,' cried the old pilot, unfurling the fingers of his good hand. 'Strange, isn't it? Yes, these very hands.'

'I hope you get better soon, Sir.'

As Arun walked away, a sense of loss overwhelmed him. Perhaps it was the state of the grounded pilot who still soared in his dreams, or was it the notion that these would be his last moments at the hospital—the sights and smells, the familiar faces, voices now, and voices lost in the corridors, never to be heard again. The wedding rings that lost their fingers, resigned expressions of hope and despair, the fading sounds of traffic down below watched by meditative pigeons perched on crisscrossing electrical wires, young nurses with stolen glances—all this was about to become a memory. And, one day perhaps, he would soar in his dreams, gathering the fragments of his memory.

And then there she was—Sujata. Her face flushed as she tick-tocked her heels up the staircase. She wore tight Jodhpuri trousers as if she had just been horse riding. Arun's cheeks flushed as he did not expect to see her.

'Just came to say goodbye to you,' she said, flicking the strands of hair from her forehead. 'I am really sorry about what happened, you know, at my engagement. I hear you are flying to England tomorrow night.'

'I thought I would never get to see you again.'

'Well, well, you may see me in England because Major Dhillon might go there for deputation next year. That is if he does not change his mind about marrying me. He is really embarrassed by my mother's psychotic episodes.'

'How is Vinod?'

'Oh, he really misses your book readings. His vision is almost nil now.'

'Have you decided what you will do next?'

'I am going to work for a non-government organization helping war widows. Yes, in this very town, my beloved Dehradun. Write to me,' she said, wiping her eyes, and then turned toward the stairs. After a few steps, the clicking of her heels stopped momentarily, and then he could hear the echo again.

24

At the mission compound, the banyan tree—with its brooding aerial roots, defying aging, timeless in uncertainty—stood steadfast. Under its dark shade, Arun felt like a fleeting shadow, never to return again to this edge of heaven. Victoria watched him drag his suitcase, his only possession, across the lawn to the bungalow. She opened the wire-mesh door with a smile.

He was out of breath. 'How did the meeting go with the Bishop?' he asked anxiously.

'I have another five years in India, or perhaps less if they change the rules, which they seem to do ever so frequently,' she replied, pouring tea, her favourite blend of Earl Grey and Darjeeling. 'The Bishop said the VHPs and BJPs, and God knows who else, are now calling the missionaries "CIA operatives". Would you like a cup of tea?'

'Yes, please.'

'I guess people will call you names if you are a foreigner no matter what country you are in. In Britain, I am afraid they will call you names. But the irony is that when you return to India after a few years, you will feel like a stranger in your own homeland.'

'Do you feel like a stranger when you go back home?'

'Absolutely. Britain is changing, just as India is changing. Nothing remains quite the same, except our memories, I suppose, which is good in a way.' She opened the rosewood chest of drawers with its brass handles. She handed him a sleek wooden box that had a framed copy of Psalm 23 in her handwriting. The box smelled of rosewood and lavender.

'Something for you for troubled times, and to remember your time here. I wish I could come and see you off in Delhi, but I have commitments here. Trishna will be here later, and she does want to travel with you to Delhi. All I can say, Arun, is this—tell her what you mean in your heart of hearts.'

'I understand. I am not sure myself what life has in store for me. Thanks for everything, and for everything you have done for me. It has been more than what I deserve. I hope to see you when you come to England.'

'Yes, of course,' she said with a quiver in her voice. She gave him a quick embrace and turned away to conceal her tear-filled eyes.

Arun walked towards the kitchen to say goodbye to John. He had prepared cheese-and-tomato sandwiches, wrapped in oiled paper, for the train journey to Delhi. He stood in his apron with downcast eyes. Ramu sat in a corner trying to learn the English alphabet. 'Have a safe journey, Doctor Sahib. I have put crushed black pepper in this paper separately; there is some fruit and a small flask of tea in this bag.'

Arun clasped his hands. They felt bony and cold. The apron seemed to swallow his dwindling frame. 'Thank you, John, for everything you have done for me. I will miss your cooking in England. Please accept this small gift from me,' said Arun, pulling out some notes from his pocket.

'Oh no, Sahib. I do not need any money. You know, I will only spend it on cigarettes.'

Arun put the cash in John's pocket anyway. 'When do you leave for the Valley of Flowers?'

'In a few days, God willing, as soon as the mountain passes have opened.'

Arun picked up the food. He held John by his shoulders and said: 'I will miss you and Miss Sahib very much.'

When Arun came out of the kitchen, he saw Trishna with a small suitcase, talking to Victoria. What surprised him was her appearance. He had never seen her wearing jeans. Her eyes were bloodshot and swollen as if she had not slept.

'Hello, Trishna. You do look different,' said Arun.

'Why, don't you like my jeans?'

'I do. It's just that I have always seen you in Indian clothes.'

'Well, everyone wears jeans in Delhi. You should know that,' she said with a little annoyance in her voice.

'She looks gorgeous, Arun. Look, I have a meeting soon in the school. I don't want to see you walk away from here. You have a safe journey and you'll be in my thoughts and prayers. Promise you will write to me and Trishna as soon as you can.' She gave him another hug and walked away with brisk strides down the pathway to the school without waving back at him.

The black Ambassador taxi drove past the litchi grove and his apartment in the mission compound, and then with the grating noise of the tyres on the gravel, it made a right turn onto the main road to Astley Hall. Arun and Trishna did not speak to each other, engrossed in their thoughts. The sound of blowing horns from the traffic in front and behind was almost soothing. The hospital came into view. Within its walls were the familiar voices, the hands he had touched, and the faces he would never see again, like the fighter pilot who lay there paralyzed, the patients whose bodies and minds had betrayed them, and the look of hope only human eyes can display.

The railway platform was littered with the bedrolls and holdalls of the Army cadets and soldiers. The steam train to Delhi glided out of the platform curving towards the Shivalik range in the distance. Soon the ramparts of the city and clustered human dwellings gave way to lush green fields. Arun stared out of the window as little villages sped past: the misshapen red-brick houses with flat roofs, where clotheslines swayed in the bright sunlight and women sat cross-legged, surrounded by trays of drying chilies. Here some of the children would go blind from vitamin A deficiency, become disabled with rickets, die of simple dehydration after intestinal infections, and their mothers would die in childbirth.

❖

Trishna intended to spend the night with her cousin at the nurse's hostel at Wellingdon Hospital after seeing off Arun at the airport. The flight was at an ungodly hour, late into the early hours of the morning.

'What are you thinking?' she asked him, holding his hands.

'Just life,' he shrugged.

'Not about me?'

'I think about you all the time.'

'I will wait for you, if you want me to, Arun.' She leaned her head against his shoulder, 'But I also want what is the best for you.'

He squeezed her hand and kissed her on the cheek, his lips moistened by her solitary tear. There was very little traffic after midnight, until they reached the airport. Passengers in shiny suits, garlanded with marigold flowers, stood triumphantly amongst the family members and well-wishers, crowding the waiting area as if there was a wedding. Other passengers in traditional clothing stood in clusters as if they were waiting at their village bus stop.

Arun held her by the arms and drew her to his chest. Putting his arms around her back, he said: 'Will you wait for me? I will write to you as soon as I get there.'

'I will wait as long as you want me to.' They kissed each other and then he walked away.

'I will be at the visitor's gallery upstairs,' she yelled after him as she began to sob.

Separated by the glass wall, there was sudden quietness in the great hall, except for the echoes of the walking shoes. He wanted to look at the visitor's gallery to see if she was still there, but he kept walking. He stopped suddenly and looked up. She was still there with the bewildered look of Eurydice, until she was swallowed by the waving arms of the Hadean crowd behind the glass wall.

❖

On the plane, people talked in soft voices. The air smelled different. He wanted to close his eyes and fall asleep. Sitting next to him, an Indian man in a suit, speaking with an American accent, summoned an air hostess. The air hostesses, with slender midriffs wrapped in maroon-coloured saris, spoke in English, sort of polished English.

'May I help you, Sir?' she asked with a bow.

'I want a Jack Daniels with Coke.'

'And what would you like to drink, Sir?' she asked Arun with a smile. He considered his choice for a few seconds, and then he thought, why not? 'I would like to have a beer.'

The air hostess appeared in the cabin like a mirage out of the Arabian Nights at this time of the morning, seeming so fresh and radiant in the subdued light. 'That would be two dollars, Sir,' she said, handing Arun the beer. He made a quick currency conversion and took out his rupees. He really did not want to spend the twenty-pound note Victoria had given him.

The air hostess smiled at him. 'Sir, we only accept dollars or pounds.'

Arun felt deflated. 'I am traveling by the national airline of India. Why do I have to pay in foreign currency?'

'I am sorry, Sir. It is the airline's rule.'

'In that case, I would prefer to have water.'

'With or without ice, Sir?'

The man in the suit interjected. 'I will pay for it. Please give him the beer.'

'It is okay. I am fine,' said Arun.

'No, no, it is my pleasure. Please have it and give me company. Travelling for the first time?'

'Yes, indeed. To London. And you?'

'To New York.'

The middle-aged man owned businesses in New York. Arun told him he was going to London to take the entrance exam for the National Health Service. 'In that case, you must have more beer. They call it "lager" over there, and drink a lot of it.'

Arun looked out of the window. The sun lit up the bare landscape of the Middle East. Flames erupted from the reddish earth in flares, presumably from the oil fields. The beer seemed too strong for him. He leaned against the window and fell asleep.

He was nudged by the air hostess to sit upright and put on his seat belt as they were about to land in London. Excitedly, he looked out of the window and saw the grey slate roofs of London in neat rows and semicircles. The roads bisected little townships with geometric designs, and a great grey sky stretched towards the horizon, where the green fields merged with the sky. Then the meandering river, which looked equally grey, lit up momentarily like molten mercury in the slanted sunlight. There was an order and symmetry in contrast to the landscape of his homeland, uneven and chaotic, shrouded in dust and haze.

Everything seemed quiet at the airport. There were no milling crowds. The corridors gleamed in the filtered weak sunlight from the giant glass walls. But then there was a surprise. The floors were being mopped by hefty Punjabi women with heavy gold bangles and nose rings. They merrily chatted with each other in Punjabi. They wore traditional clothes, not uniforms. Arun avoided their gaze and quickly walked past them, suppressing a feeling of empathy and disgust. They seemed happy enough.

At the luggage belt, he quickly spotted his small canvas suitcase which consisted mostly of textbooks. Perhaps it was the smallest suitcase. To his horror, he saw it was covered in oil. Someone's canister of pickles must have leaked mustard oil with its odious pungent smell. He worried that his books and few clothes would be stained with the golden yellow oil, reeking of spices.

As soon as he walked out of Customs, he saw his mother standing with his younger brother. He had suddenly grown into a tall young man. His mother gave him a broad smile with welcoming arms. He noticed she had two front teeth missing. She looked much older with her spray of grey hair.

'Welcome to England,' said his brother with a big hug, and almost lifted him off the floor. 'Wait 'til you see my Volkswagen van that I use for work.'

'I thought you were in the last year of school.'

'I am. I sell anoraks at the markets over the weekend.'

The van was several years old and painted orange in colour. They drove out of the airport onto the motorway to Manchester, which cut through the English countryside. The icy rain mixed with snow followed them all the way until they reached the outskirts of Manchester, where a big procession was blocking the traffic. 'Who are these people?' asked Arun.

'These are called the skinheads—you see their shaved heads? They belong to the National Front Party, and they want us out of the country.'

His brother swerved the van to take a detour. A skinhead with tattooed arms cocked his head towards the window. From his stained teeth, he squirted a jet of spit that splattered the window. He shouted: 'You, Paki.'

'That is what they call us. Pakistanis!'

25

When the saffron-clad crowd gathered outside the mission compound carrying placards denouncing conversions to Christianity, Victoria clutched her Bible and locked herself in her bedroom. She called Mr Gupta in a panic, which swept her to her childhood memory of the Blitz of London. But there was a difference. Here, she could see the enemy, like some ancient tribe with poles and shields, lurking under the canopy of fruit trees in front of the bungalow.

She opened the Bible to Isaiah, chapter 41, verse 10, and read to herself: *Fear thou not; for I am with thee: be not dismayed for I am thy God: I will help thee; yea, I will uphold thee with the right hand of my righteousness.*

'Don't you worry,' Mr Gupta said in a calm voice. 'I will be there with a truckload of workers from the quarry in a few minutes. These people of the right-wing political party have been emboldened by their landslide victory. Just stay indoors.'

'I will. I have locked myself in the bedroom. When you come, please come in from the kitchen. John is there. The police are taking an awful long time,' she said, getting out of breath.

There were only fifteen to twenty people in the crowd. Their chants became louder as they neared the bungalow. She parted the curtains of her bedroom window and got a glimpse of their leader, a man of average height with a black flowing beard and his hair tied in a bun. His sinewy arms rose up and down like a wound-up tin toy. She pulled her dresser against the door, securing her garrison, and began to pray.

After what seemed like an eternity, from the reflection in the mirror of her dresser, she saw a dusty truck pull up with bare brown bodies covered in white cement ash. They jumped out of the truck, followed by Mr Gupta in a suit. He walked to confront the leader of the group with a cowboyish confidence. Soon the crowd melted away, leaving the placards under the trees. The police jeeps arrived soon after to inspect the property.

Mr Gupta entered through the kitchen door at the back of the house. Victoria regained her composure. John, in his staid manner, brought in two glasses of water. 'Thank the Lord you arrived at the right time. This has never happened before, never in all the years I have been in Dehradun,' Victoria said softly, dabbing her eyes.

'Do you really think it was about religion?'

'Didn't you see the placards they were carrying?'

Mr Gupta took a sip of ice-cold water. 'Of course, I saw the placards. But that is not the real reason. You see, this church property is prime land for the newly elected politicians. They want to scare you so that one day they can grab the property. I know the system here. But one good thing the British left behind was an independent judiciary, so don't you worry.'

'I was so scared. I wish Arun was here.'

'You do miss him a lot, don't you?'

Victoria sat down near the window and gazed at the lush green lawn. 'I suppose I do miss him in a way. This place doesn't feel the same anymore.' She turned her face towards him. 'I really do not want to live in this compound anymore, but I don't want to leave Dehradun.'

Mr Gupta stepped closer to her and took her hand. He looked into her sparkling blue eyes and said: 'You don't ever have to leave Dehradun. This is where you belong.'

'For me, belonging is where God wants me, and living is where your heart is, I suppose. This is becoming a strange land for me.'

'Nothing is strange where your heart is.'

Victoria was petrified to stay alone in the bungalow that night. She kept staring at the apartment, now looking ghostly. There were no open windows, or the towels or laundry drying in the balcony.

'Would you like to stay for supper?'

'I shall be delighted with your company.'

'Thank you for taking care of me. I really don't know what I would have done.'

Ravi, Mr Gupta's cousin, heard about the incident. He picked up Trishna from her apartment and drove her to see Victoria. The four of them talked late into the night and played Scrabble in front of the wood fire. Victoria brought a tray of walnuts with a silver-plated nutcracker. She handed the tray to Ravi. 'You can crack the walnuts. You have strong hands.'

'I have horrible letters. I can't make up a word,' said Trishna contemplatively.

Ravi watched the golden light of the flames dance on Trishna's face. He forgot it was his turn to make a word. The walnut shells crackled in the fire, giving off short starry flickers of flame. The bungalow was aglow with camaraderie and laughter once again—for the first time since Arun's departure.

26

When his mother's blue-coloured aerogrammes used to arrive at the mission compound from England, bearing stamps with the crowned portrait of the Queen or the House of Commons, Arun had imagined the address 48 Greenwood House as a little house with a garden. A small garden perhaps, pocket-handkerchief gardens as they called them. To his surprise, the address turned out to be a monstrous, four-storey, grimy brick building silhouetted against the purple sky and what seemed like a prolonged twilight from the golden yellow lights of the city of *Munchuster*, as his mother called it. The building stood at some elevation, and the city lights glimmered like jewels as far as the eye could see.

'I have to park my van here so that I can see it from my bedroom window on the fourth floor. There are a lot of Irish thieves here. They have a name for everything; they call them "Paddies",' said his brother, trying to orient him to this new world.

'From the photographs you sent me, I thought you lived somewhere else,' protested Arun with a tone of indignation.

'Yes, I know, I know. We were, but when Dad was disrespectful to our mother, I threatened to hit him. He called the police and moved out. We had no money for the rent, so the social services have given us this council apartment.'

'Why did you never tell me about all this?'

He could hear his mother sobbing at the back. As they walked towards the staircase lit with a dingy electric bulb, the stench of urine, discarded beer bottles, and dampness pervaded the staircase. The brick walls were scribbled with obscenities and swastikas. Shiny candy wrappers floated like tinsel in the cold wind that swept up as if in a chimney. This was an unimagined world, a shock to the senses, as Robert Clive must have felt when he first set his eyes upon the streets and alleys of Calcutta. A world so far removed from the land of Shakespeare and Wordsworth. Where were those daffodils? Surely, this was not the England of his imagination, the land of great explorers and inventors, of the great kings and queens who ruled the earth.

His younger siblings had been waiting patiently for his arrival. As soon as the door opened, they pounced upon him, another younger brother and two sisters. They all seemed to have grown into teenagers. The kerosene fumes from the portable heaters stung his eyes. He began to cry, but to his family he said, 'It's just the fumes.' His eyes wandered, as if surveying a cell to look for some signs of comfort, a mattress or a washing sink. His siblings spoke in a strange accent he had never heard before. The youngest sister said to his brother, 'You whaaat, shove off.'

While the others somehow managed to rest for the night in one room, Arun had the other small room with a bed to himself. The sheets felt damp and cold. The fumes from the heaters permeated everything. He was too exhausted to think. His mind raced back and forth to the images of the mission compound and his own accommodation. He wished he was back in India in the bed he had slept in for so long.

As night fell, the stillness was broken with sirens of police cars from some distant road. Arun could not sleep. His eyes watered, and he himself did not know if he was crying in his sleep or if it was a mere allergy to the fumes. He pulled open the curtains and saw the lights of the city spread out like golden necklaces, as if paradise lay elsewhere. As if he was sitting on a wall between heaven and hell. The window frosted as soon as he wiped it. He lay down in his bed again and turned towards the wall, which seemed to have turned white. That can't be true, he thought, and then it occurred to him to scratch it with his finger nails. He scratched his name on the film of ice that had formed inside the room.

He woke up with a splitting headache. His mother made toast with melted yellow cheese for breakfast, and then left for work at the nearby garment factory. His siblings had left for school. He lay there staring at the cracks in the ceiling.

A tap was dripping somewhere in the kitchen, breaking the bleak silence of a cold and empty apartment. He pulled his suitcase from under the bed. The pages of the textbook of medicine had macerated, soaked by spicy pickle oil that had sat under an Indian sun. The box Victoria had given was somehow intact. He opened it and took out the frame. He read out Psalm 23 aloud to himself: *The Lord is my shepherd and I shall not want*... He put the frame on the stand next to his bed.

There was no telephone in the apartment. He did see a pay phone outside the building, but he did not want to get out of the bed, let alone the apartment. All of a sudden, his world seemed to have contracted. He felt like a formless genie who could see the outside world from the confines of the bottle, aware of the possibilities, once freed, of green pastures and still waters, but for now he must keep gathering himself perpetually in his shrinking abode and only dream of what he had left behind. He prayed to the

Lord to grant him the patience of a genie and its power when freed.

The library was three miles away in the town centre. The bus ride would cost a pound each way. He possessed only a twenty-pound note. Three miles would be a piece of cake for him. He walked on Longsight Road which took him into the town centre. A man in a dirty overcoat began to follow him to the entrance of the library. He coughed and spat a blob of yellow phlegm on the pavement. 'Could you spare me a quid for some cigarettes, mate?'

'Sorry, I don't smoke.' Arun fumbled and pulled his pockets inside out, 'I am sorry, truly sorry.'

'Who cares if you don't smoke, you fucker.'

Arun hurried into the library, embracing its warmth under the great dome of hushed voices. The walk back seemed much longer than three miles. A cold wind was blowing in his ears. The sky had turned silvery grey, just enough to cast shadows but light enough to silhouette the elegant buildings. When he reached Greenwood House it began to drizzle. The sky turned a darker blue, and then suddenly an empty milk bottle came flying from the floors above him and shattered into pieces at his feet. When he looked up, he could only see the yellow lights of the dirty windows.

27

Arun lay in bed all day. The apartment was so cold that his bones felt chilled. The sky was grey with drizzling gusts of icy rain tapping the window now and then. The inefficient kerosene heater gave off more fumes than heat. When the postman dropped some letters through the door he jumped out of the bed, grabbed the mail and jumped back into bed again.

He recognized Trishna's handwriting on one of the envelopes. Another letter was from the General Medical Council of London. He quickly opened the letter from London, which informed him he had passed the written exam and that the oral exam would be held in Edinburgh the following week. He jumped out of bed again and stretched his arms in glee in front of the heater. He wished there would be lightning in the sky, but there was only the constant nagging drizzle to dampen the spirit, and there were no storms here to hold you in awe like the ones he had experienced in India after a hot summer's day.

He opened Trishna's letter which seemed bulky, as if the envelope was not large enough for the paper. The pages were numbered, and each page had an Om inscribed in Hindi on the top.

My dearest Arun,

After I left you at the airport I stood watching you from the barrier for a long time, even after you were gone. You only turned once to look in my direction, and I am not sure if you saw me waving back at you. I decided not to stay with my cousin in the hostel. I took a taxi to the railway station and boarded the train to Dehradun which left at five in the morning. When I got to Dehradun it was raining very hard and my HMT watch, which you bought for me, got wet in the rain and stopped working at precisely nine-thirty a.m., when I got off the train.

I thought I would take it for repair several times, but every time I took it to the repair shop, I turned back as I wanted the time to stay at nine-thirty to remind me of the time I left you. I will only repair it when you return, or if we are together again.

It is four weeks since you left. I do not feel like going to the mission compound, but I would like to see Victoria more often. Last week, when I saw her we talked about you and we both burst into tears. I know you are studying hard for your exams, so I understand you have not written to me for so long. I will only write to you again if I hear from you. I hope you are studying hard for your exams. I am praying for your success.

Tears began to well up in his eyes. He closed his eyes and imagined he was back in the mission compound. He could hear the sound of the wind in the banyan tree. He stopped reading the letter. Yes, he must pass his exams. The oral exam was equally important, if not more, as he would have to face an English physician across the table. The exam was going to be held at the Royal College of Physicians in Edinburgh. If he did not pass the oral exam, he would fail the entire exam.

He wondered what Scotland would be like. Would it be as dreary as Manchester, with defunct chimneys under overcast skies and abandoned warehouses? Or would it be a city of the Great Empire as he had imagined? After all, it had the Royal College of Physicians?

The following week, he took the train from Manchester. It rolled through the graffiti-covered tunnels and under the bridges with swastikas to the beautiful rolling hills of Cumbria, dotted with farms. The green fields hugged the slopes with their stone boundaries. A blue lake, almost as blue as the sky, shimmered in the lap of two mountains, and suddenly he felt he was in the land of Wordsworth.

He found a bed-and-breakfast place near Queens Street, walking distance from the Royal College. The Scottish landlady, with a husky voice from years of smoking, handed him the key to a room with a single bed and a tiny window. Pointing to the slot in the wall, she said, 'Yeah haav to put a tuppence in the metre for the hoat shower.'

What she did not tell him was that a tuppence would only give enough time to lather. He did not have another tuppence, so the only choice was to have a cold shower or to wipe off the soap suds with a towel. He got ready for the viva voce and took a brisk walk in the wind that swept in from the Highlands, to cobbled streets lined with Gothic buildings, blackened by the city's smoke. He found the pillared entrance to the college.

Once inside, he was struck by its grandiosity. He could almost smell knowledge. A grand mahogany staircase, with wood panelling to the ceiling, adorned with portraits of famous English and Scottish physicians with sombre countenances, led to the great hall. As he climbed the stairs, he had the petrified expression of Alice in Wonderland, and he was almost breathless by the time he reached the table. Sitting behind it were two elderly examiners in striped suits and gold-rimmed glasses that rested upon their bushy white eyebrows. They eyed him with a measured gaze.

'Have a seat, will you?' said one of them authoritatively.

'Where are you from, if I may ask?'

'From India, Sir.'

'Whereabouts in India?'

'From northern India, Sir. Err…from the foothills of the Himalayas,' Arun blurted nervously.

'Aaa-ha! Interesting. Darjeeling?'

The other examiner gave a wry smile and asked his colleague, 'Flynn, wasn't your grandfather a tea planter in Darjeeling?'

'Yes, indeed.'

This introduction made Arun feel a little at ease but not enough to stop the palpitations and the bead of sweat that broke on his upper lip.

The examiner with the India connection leaned forward and said in a quiet yet playful voice, 'Imagine you are sailing off the coast of Indonesia as a ship's doctor with your captain, and you are quietly drinking a gin and tonic, enjoying a beautiful sunset and suddenly someone from the boiler room comes up and says, "There is a sailor lying unconscious on the floor." What would you do, Doctor?' The examiner leaned back into his plush, velvety chair and took off his glasses and carefully folded them on the table, giving Arun some time to think.

'The first thing I would do is to remove the sailor from the heat of the boiler room.'

The two examiners looked at each other and nodded. 'That seems reasonable,' one of them said. 'You have transported him to the exam room, then what would you do?'

'Sir, I will check if he is breathing, his pulse, BP and his temperature, which might give me a clue about heat exhaustion.'

'Well, his pulse is 110, BP 90/60 and temperature 104.'

Arun quickly tried to narrow his choices in his mind to determine the cause of the sailor's unconsciousness. 'Sir, history is very important to provide some clues to ascertain the cause. I would ask the people in the boiler room if he had a fall, causing a head injury, or if he had a seizure or if he was taking any drugs.'

'He was a healthy sailor and he had none of those things. I presume you gave him some fluids and cold compresses. He remains unconscious, and the captain is very worried about losing his engineer.'

Arun could feel the muscles of his forehead tighten up like a clasp around his head. 'Sir, I would then check his blood sugar, in case he has very low sugar.'

'It is normal. I told you he was perfectly healthy and had no history of diabetes.'

'If there is an ophthalmoscope on the ship, I would like to check his fundi for any haemorrhages, for any signs of cerebro-vascular accident.'

The other examiner nodded in agreement. Arun felt a little better, but his tongue was heavy and dry as leather. The examiner leaned forward again and said, 'All that is normal. His temperature is down with cold compresses. What is the matter with him?'

Arun looked up at the blue ceiling with ornate gold patterns in between the beams of the great hall. He was almost in a reverie until the examiner boomed. 'The man is still unconscious!'

The other examiner laughed and said, 'The candidate or the sailor, Flynn?'

The examiner with a sense of humour asked Arun if he had to make a choice, what instruments he would like to take on board the ship.

'I would like to take a thermometer, BP instrument, an ophthalmoscope and equipment for basic lab work.'

'Anything else?'

'Maybe a microscope.'

'Aaa-ha!' said the examiner with the India connection. 'And what would you do with a microscope?'

'Sir, look at blood films.'

'And what might you see on this man's blood film?'

It was as if Arun had navigated through a dark tunnel and suddenly he could see the light. 'A malaria parasite!'

The examiner's face lit up with a smile that was fleeting. The facial lines reappeared as soon as he stopped smiling. 'It was cerebral malaria. I am afraid you took too long to diagnose him, Doctor. Your patient died, I am afraid. Thank you for coming to the Royal College of Physicians.'

As Arun walked away, his mind still reeling under the spell of the tropics, swaying like a ship off the coast of Indonesia, he faced the chill winds of the Scottish highlands. Why could he not think about malaria when he himself would have died from it had John not found him in his apartment? He knew his name would not be on the list of successful candidates. The examiner had indeed given him hints of gin and tonic and malaria. Why did he not see the connection? He had been thinking like an Englishman. Being in a temperate country, somehow, the tropical diseases seemed low on his list.

He walked on the cobbled streets toward Edinburgh Castle on the hill that dominated the city's skyline. Inside the old castle, he came upon a display in a glass case that shocked him. It was the blood-stained tunic of the great Indian warrior Tipu Sultan, who had stood up valiantly against the British and died fighting. The tear in the garment was the site where the dagger had pierced his liver.

Arun stood there in homage for a long time, unable to control his tears. He felt defeated like the great warrior, but at the same time he felt inspired that he would fight his battle with the blessing of Tipu Sultan.

His name was not on that evening's list of successful candidates. The next exam would be held at Glasgow in two months. It seemed like a long time. He walked back to the Victorian station for the long ride to Manchester. What would he tell everyone? His father had disappeared and had not even bothered to contact him. Strangers on a train, he smiled to himself. He did not want to think of anyone for the next two months. An elderly couple sitting in front of him methodically unwrapped their cucumber sandwiches, and a young couple, roughly his age, were locked in a tight embrace, oblivious of anyone around them. Arun blushed instinctively.

The train whizzed past empty stations, unlike the crowded stations of India. He felt empty inside and wished he could sleep for two months until the next exam. When he reached Manchester, the bus dropped him about a mile away from the apartment building. It was three in the afternoon, but the sun had long disappeared. It was raining almost like black rain, with shiny black puddles on the road. A car passed by at high speed, splattering grimy water on his face.

When he reached home, his brother opened the door and said, 'Oh, you look like a bloody Jameeca, did you pass?'

'No,' he said. There was a hushed silence. He went into his room and slept for a long time.

❖

Two months later, he was in Glasgow, which reminded him of Manchester. He had mastered Tropical Medicine to the core. This time the examiner asked him about a young Irish woman who was tripping frequently while walking.

'Has she been to the tropics?' asked Arun.

'No, no, she has never been out of Dingle Peninsula.'

Tropics excluded, Arun quickly honed his final diagnosis into auto-immune diseases that afflict the Irish more than others. The diagnosis was Multiple Sclerosis. He had begun to think like an English physician. Elated at seeing his name in the list of candidates selected, he walked on Queen Street to the nearest pub.

28

The most peaceful time at Greenwood House, this edifice of British socialism to house the have-nots of society, was at night. The city lights shimmered from the fourth floor into the horizon. One never saw the starry sky here, just pale darkness. From the next-door apartment came the sound of ABBA's latest hit: 'Money, money, money, must be funny, in a rich man's world...' He gazed at the lights, and the cars on the motorway seemed like celestial trains zig-zagging across the landscape. He thought of the warning about materialism that Victoria had given him. This was another world, and he must rise to the challenge. From now on, he must embrace Kipling's imposters—triumph and disaster.

When the envelope bearing the embossed three-headed lions came from India, he recognized Victoria's handwriting. He had written a depressed letter to her about his failing the exam and his longing to be back in India:

I am as confused as you are—what to call home? What makes us leave our shores? Your purpose was guided by God, and mine by circumstances. Perhaps, God created circumstances for me. In a way, we are all missionaries. Our lives will touch others; in return, we will be touched by them, wherever we live.

He excitedly opened Victoria's letter, as though he was holding a piece of his homeland in his hands.

Dear Arun,

I cannot believe you have been gone for almost six months. Spring is here and I see new buds on the litchi trees. I can almost see you sitting under the banyan tree. I am sorry to know you did not get through the exam. I did have you in my thoughts and prayers, especially after reading how disheartened you felt in your present circumstances. Have faith in the Lord—you will have better days.

I did not want to write to you earlier to give you the sad news. John passed away peacefully when he reached the Valley of Flowers with his young nephew. His lungs could not take the altitude. His nephew buried him there. May he rest in peace. I do not have a full-time cook now. Ramu attends school, but he helps me a little in the kitchen. In return, I am teaching him English. You never did taste my stews. I think I have become quite an expert.

Trishna came to see me with Ravi the other day. She said she hadn't heard from you for so long. Trishna and Ravi seem very happy together. He helped her move to her new apartment. As far as I am concerned, I have decided to stay on in India. The past few months have been stressful with the changes taking place in India. Mr Gupta has been very supportive. I call him Rakesh now. Strange it may seem, I would never have met him had it not been for the saga of the wedding rings. He is a wonderful person and has found peace in Christ. He has asked me to marry him. I was surprised, of course, but I have faith that the Lord will guide me. I have asked Rakesh to give me some more time.

I wish you the best for the upcoming exam. I am sure you will do fine this time. You will be in my thoughts and prayers, as always.

Arun read the letter over and over again. *Trishna and Ravi seem very happy together...*

If only he could talk to his friend Sodi who had scolded him for being sentimental at Chakrata. But there was no friend here; only the walls of the apartment that entombed him. From the window he could see a park in the distance but, until now, he'd been afraid to walk there.

There were no banyan trees that whispered in the breeze. He held the letter as he walked. How could the HMT watch, the best watch ever made in India, that he had lovingly bought for her in Dehardun, stop? Just stop after getting wet in the rain? It was as if Time itself had stopped and she had not bothered to fix it. He sat in the park with the letter fluttering in his hands. Was Ravi walking with her in the distant litchi grove as he had once walked with her?

How empty she must have felt after dropping him off at the airport. Perhaps she knew in her heart the arms of the watch would never come together again, and she wanted to preserve that moment of parting. But time does not stop; it is the keepers of time that change. A spray of light rain, annoying yet soothing, hit his face. The rain began to soak him.

An English woman with an umbrella, walking her dog, passed him by. 'Awful weather, luv,' she said, turning her head to see if he was still on the bench.

'I love the rain!' He waved to her.

Arun walked into the Victorian building overlooking the barren hills of Lancashire, which housed the small hospital where he got his first posting. On the gleaming corridor, a young English nurse with long strides caught up with him.

'Are you the new doctor on the medical floor?'

'Yes, indeed.'

'Hello, I am Wendy,' she said, extending her hand.

'You have warm hands,' commented Arun with a smile.

'But I don't have a cold heart,' she said with a wink. 'Where are you from?'

'India.'

'You look different.'

'Why?'

'Well, most Indian doctors have a moustache, and they also have rings on their fingers because either they're married or engaged.'

'Well, I am neither.' He looked at his fingers, arching them in a strange sort of a way, turning his hand a couple of times. 'I shall never wear any rings on these fingers.'

'Why so?' she asked, looking puzzled.

'It is a rather long story. Maybe I will tell you one day. If you care to hear.'

Acknowledgements

I have always found it very difficult to say thank you because I usually don't know where to begin. I could start with my kindergarten teacher... But on a serious note, the person who has inspired me, and many others, is Mr Ruskin Bond, not only for his iconic writing but for his philosophy of life itself, which pervades his literary work.

I wish also to thank Meena Khorana for setting me on my mark and keeping me on track to complete the book; Shanti Chandrasekhar, for reading several drafts, editing and organizing the chapters; Shahid Mahmood, for listening to me read aloud the first drafts in my office; Toronney Mixon, for his insight on our long walks; Naseem Ishaque, from my college, for her encouragement; Ravi Singh, for his detailed analysis and criticism and believing in the book.

Kathryn Johnson, my critic and mentor from The Writers Center in Washington DC, thank you, for all your help and guidance. Radhika Shenoy, my wonderful editor, and her colleague, Shalini Krishan—at the other end of the world, connected by WhatsApp—for their eye for detail and valuable suggestions: thank you for bringing this to fruition.

And I mustn't forget Yash: his technical support in gleaning different versions from different computers and getting me out of the digital maze was invaluable. And, of course, thanks to my wife, who tolerated the night lamp beside our bed when I wrote, and to my daughter Sheetal, who can type faster than she can talk.

Finally, in remembrance, for Beryl, my dear friend, who sadly did not live to see the cover of this book.